THE OLD GANG

By the same Author

Novels

The Feathers of Death
Brother Cain
Doctors Wear Scarlet
September Castle
Close of Play
The Roses of Picardie
An Inch of Fortune

Alms for Oblivion Series

The Rich Pay Late
Friends in Low Places
The Sabre Squadron
Fielding Gray
The Judas Boy
Places Where They Sing
Sound the Retreat
Come Like Shadows
Bring Forth the Body
The Survivors

The First-born of Egypt Series

Morning Star
The Face of the Waters

Memoirs

Shadows on the Grass

Belles-lettres

The English Gentleman
Boys Will Be Boys
The Fortunes of Fingle
The Old School

Plays

Royal Foundation and other plays

THE OLD GANG

A Sporting and Military Memoir

by

Simon Raven

Illustrations by Tim Jaques

HAMISH HAMILTON · LONDON

HAMISH HAMILTON LTD

ESSEX COUNTY LIBRARY

Published by the Penguin Group
27 Wrights Lane, London W8 5TZ, England
Viking Penguin Inc., 40 West 23rd Street, New York, New York 10010, U.S.A.
Penguin Books Australia Ltd, Ringwood, Victoria, Australia
Penguin Books Canada Ltd, 2801 John Street, Markham, Ontario, Canada L3R 1B4
Penguin Books (N.Z.) Ltd, 182–190 Wairau Road, Auckland 10, New Zealand

Penguin Books Ltd, Registered Offices: Harmondsworth, Middlesex, England

First Published in Great Britain 1988 by
Hamish Hamilton Ltd

Text copyright © 1988 by Simon Raven
Illustrations copyright © 1988 by Tim Jaques

British Library Cataloguing in Publication Data

Raven, Simon
    The old gang.
    1. Raven, Simon—Biography   2. Authors,
    English—20th century—Biography
    I. Title
    823'.914   PR6068.A9Z/

ISBN 0–241–12283–X

Typeset and printed by Butler & Tanner Ltd, Frome, Somerset

GENTLE READER, pray remember:

If you so wished [said Parlamente] we could go each afternoon between midday and four o'clock to the lovely meadow that borders the Gave de Pau, where the leaves on the trees are so thick that the hot sun cannot penetrate the shade and the cool beneath. There we can sit and rest, and each of us will tell a story which he has either witnessed himself, or which he had heard from somebody worthy of belief.... But if any of you is able to think of something more agreeable, I shall gladly bow to his or her opinion.

From the Prologue to The Heptameron
(trans. P. A. Chilton, Penguin)

'If a man, when he has heard or seen or in any other way perceived a thing, knows not only that thing, but also has a perception of some other thing, the knowledge of which is not the same, but different, are we not right in saying that he recollects the thing of which he has the perception?'

'What do you mean?'

'Let me give you an example. Knowledge of a man is different from knowledge of a lyre?'

'Of course.'

'Well, you know that a lover, when he sees a lyre or a cloak or anything else which his lover is wont to use, perceives the lyre and, in his mind, receives an image of the boy to whom the lyre belongs? But this is *recollection*, just as, when one sees Simmias, one often remembers Cebes. I could cite endless such examples.'

'To be sure you could,' said Simmias.

Plato, Phaedo, 18C, ll. 7–21

New Year's Day 1987

John Basil Budden (henceforward JBB) and his son, James, arrive with the rosy fingered dawn to scoop me up and most of my breakker. Hey chums for Cheltenham. Only four hours from Walmer these days, along a handsome motorway – though this much cluttered by the mechanised jacquerie and (far worse) by white-collar cits in their Sierras.

Entrance money to Cheltenham now so stiff that they have to accept Access; but at least when you get in you find the enclosure more or less free of the sneak thieves, pimps and whores that infest courses nearer London, though not, alas, free of jabbering bogmen and their smelly priests.

Decent luncheon available (soup or H. d'O.s plus roast and pud for eight and a half Bradburies): for once the caterers have got it right – but don't nobody tell 'em or they'll go and fuck it up tomorrow. Also to be had are hot beef sandwiches from a stall by the Members' Tote Credit counter at two quid a time.

Warmed up with a bite of grub, both James and JBB (old

1

enough to know better) get excited by the pubescent county girls on exhibition. I improvised fantasy about J.'s two favourite female jockeys. The wretched boy goes crosseyed with lust, but is luckily not too distracted to spot very decent odds (12 to 1) against Loddon Lad and grabs the price with three fivers in cash. Rushing to Jackie Cohen to collect loot after the race, J. stamps on foot of grotty salesman specimen with clone moustache, who sees J.'s OT tie and spits at him with, 'I know your sort – public school vermin'. J. sorts him out by wishing him a nose-crushing dose of the great pox (rather an old-fashioned curse in these days of AIDS), and is punished later when all the rest of his selections finish furlongs down the course, 'wanking', in his chosen metaphor.

Still, a quiet count shows a spot of cash in hand (though a bad day on the credit books) as the party proceeds through gloaming to M5 and M6 and so to Penrith and Major Vitreus Clere-Story's hospitable house nearby. JJB lays 25 to 1 against appearance of (genuine) caviar at dinner: taken both by J. and self for a sovereign each.

Jolly reception by Vitreus (Vity) and his wife, Vanushka, who announce that the place is heaving with visitors: so that JJB and James must share a bed ('Bugger: Father snores like a wet fart and farts like a wet snore'), and I myself must sleep in refrigerated slavvy's box about a furlong from the loo. Inconvenience somewhat compensated for by colourful quality and character (good *or* bad) of other guests: e.g. Brigadier-General Noah Pavey, one of the last few men in England to have held the rank of Brigadier-General as opposed to that of plain Brigadier, *quondam* of the 9th Lancers, and the chap who sliced his ball so vilely on the first tee at St. Andrew's that it absolutely went backwards (what with a blazing north-wester) through the club house window and nearly killed Neville Cardus. (What a pity it

'I know your sort – public school vermin'

didn't: the brute went on droning away about cricket for another generation – no wonder the game nearly died on its feet in the 'sixties.)

Also present, Beatty Belhampton (née Beri Kumangi), the old Oxonian Princess from Boganda, as Black as Boudin and twice as gamy, the women's magazine whizz girl, the one who *might* have disposed of her second hubby by 'inadvertently' shoving him down the steps of the cellar and into the rack of Taylor '27. Beatty tells a tasteless tale before dinner about a tart who gives a chap a gobble and then turns up, cheeks bulging, at the reception desk of the Spermatozoa Bank, hoping to double her fee: a good imitation by Beatty of the tart trying to talk business with her mouth full.

Also *in situ*: Milesy Malbruges, the backgammon champ, deep and dedicated punter; while Lucrezia Lippit, the intellectual Labrador breeder, now of Cumberland but by birth of the American Colonies, has come over from her Labrador hutch for dinner and a bit of a wet.

JBB very put out when caviar is served with iced vodka for the first course at dinner, Beluga at that. He now owes a pony to James and me both.

Talk turns on Cheltenham this pm. Fierce diatribe by me on the poor quality of people admitted to the club enclosure, now that it is no longer required of non-members to show a letter of introduction from one of the stewards or the secretary of their London club. How much better ordered the thing was thirty years ago (with all those mouthing hedge priests firmly wired off in Tatt's). I was then somehow diverted from this urgent social thesis and found myself launched into the tale of what passed during the first meeting (1956) which I ever attended at Cheltenham ... the appalling affair of Brindle and her Jack: –

In those days I was a soldier (I told the company at Vanushka's table) and had just returned from Kenya to my regimental depot in Shropshire, whence I was released for the three weeks' furlough due to me on disembarkation. So I put up at the old East India and Sports Club in St. James's Square and cast about for a good companion to come with me to the big March meeting (Gold Cup and the rest) at Cheltenham. Unfortunately my great regimental chum, Major O. Paradore, was still running his intelligence centre-cum-casino-cum-bawdy-house near Lake Naivasha, so no joy of him this time out. But as luck – very ill luck – would have it there was a distant cousin of O.'s also staying in the club. As even worse luck would have it I knew him very slightly, having been on the touchline when he fell down dead drunk on a colour presentation parade in Brunswick, in front of Field Marshal the Lord Harding. Jack Lofting the bloody man was called. O. had introduced me to him after the parade, while he was in his room under close arrest, escorted by some silly simpering subaltern and a case of Teacher's. Worst luck of all, I was too stupid to remind myself that a chap who falls down full of juice in front of Field Marshals at colour parades really will not do. I am not a prig in such matters but I should certainly have grasped, by then, that there are (after all) limits. The trouble was, you see, that I was rather fascinated by Jack Lofting, because he had somehow wangled his way out of the Army without being court-martialled – a particularly phony resignation, O. used to say, achieved by putting the screws on some eminent but delinquent staff wallah whom Jack could apparently prove had (a) embezzled a whole season's prize money from the funds of the BAOR Race Club and (b) used to pick up ten-year-old German boys (in *Lederhosen*) during his lone rides through Dortmund Forest and give them educational trips on his crupper. So one way and the other (O. said) the thing had been so deftly handled that Jack Lofting had been

5

allowed to resign honourably (i.e. not on pain of disgrace, or not officially so) and to remain a member of all his clubs and whatever. People still thought a good deal of those sort of things back in the 'fifties. Her Majesty the Queen, who had been informed about the pantomime at Brunswick, was said to have been livid at the let-off.

And now here was Jack in the Sports Club rearing to go to Cheltenham – and here was I, like the ninny I was in those days, so dazzled by the way he had conned himself out of the Service with white hands and a pension, that I was rearing, or at least ready, to go with him.

'One thing, my deari-o,' Jack Lofting said, 'we'll have to take Brindle Lark. My girlfriend. She's Welsh, you see, and the size of the Achilles Statue, and if we don't take her she'll find us out and crush us to powder.'

'Anything you say, Jack,' says I. Jesus, what a tit I was then.

'Okay,' he says, 'We'll go in Brindle's car. Make the great cow contribute something for once in her life. If I arrange that, and a tank of petrol on tick to get us on the road, will you fix the rooms? There's a jolly decent pub in Moreton-on-the-Marsh, and several in Broadway and Evesham.'

So I arranged a double room for 'Mr. and Mrs. Lofting', and a single for myself, and paid a hefty deposit, at The Sign of the Scholar Gipsy ten miles from the course along the Evesham Road; and presented myself at Brindle's flat in Artillery Mansions at noon on the day before the meeting started, ready to be driven down in time for dinner.

Now, Jack was a squat and chunky fifteen stoner of five-and-a-half foot and twenty-nine years: Brindle was a quivering ogress of forty steaming summers. It followed for a start that there wasn't much room for me (six foot and thickening fast). We were all three meant to be sitting on the bench seat of one of those old sporting Triumph Roadsters.

'You go in the middle,' Jack said, shoving me in next to Brindle and then crushing me against her till I crackled (like a cockroach I once killed with a chamber pot in a seedy *pensione* in Naples).

And off we went.

Off we went, that is, as far as The Volunteer in Chester Row, where it was decreed by Brindle that we should take an early luncheon. Sitting by Brindle in a maliciously angular cubicle while Jack ordered the luncheon (two quintuple gins and tonic for them, and a glass of white venom with a round of meat loaf sandwich for me) I now had my first chance to assess her extraordinary but not unattractive turnout. Brindle was dressed in a costume (skirt and jacket) of green checks, with thick orange stockings and galumphing black brogues, a white shirt with a hard collar (rounded at the points) and a Free Forester tie.

'How,' I said, 'did you come to be a Free Forester?'

'Founders' Kin,' said Brindle.

Now indeed there was (and is) a system whereby descendants of the Founder of the Free Foresters can be made members of the club, automatically or at least without formality, at the age of eighteen; but I had yet to hear that it operated in favour of females, and so I now said.

'Very simple,' said Brindle. 'Uncle Ethelred was on the committee. He fudged a cousinship with the Founder for me, and insisted that girls were not specifically excluded by the regulations – which they weren't because they'd never even been thought of.'

'Why go to all the trouble?'

'I liked the colours,' said Brindle. 'I often wear the blazer in the summer. As for Uncle Ethelred, I blackmailed him. He once took a very big liberty when I was twelve, in the back of his Daimler. Mind you, I rather enjoyed the liberty, but I didn't see why I shouldn't turn it to account.'

7

'What do you do if anyone challenges you when you're wearing the tie ... or the blazer?'

'Relics of my late husband, I tell 'em ... who was bashed in the balls by a beamer. That shuts 'em up.'

'*Beamers* don't bash you in the balls. They conk you on the napper.'

'Thank you very much for the tip. I'll emend my speech for the future.'

Jack arrived with the lunch. I ate it. They drank and prolonged it. We left at three. At half-past four (still well this side of Henley) they insisted on stopping at a friendly hostelry for 'tea'. At seven o'clock, desperate, I engaged a taxi, and having with some difficulty persuaded Brindle to release my luggage from her boot ('What's all the rush, sweetie-pie?' she said) I fled for The Sign of the Scholar Gipsy on the Cheltenham–Evesham road ... where I dined late but well (a very difficult thing to do in those days), congratulated myself on my escape, and arranged a hired car to take me to and from Cheltenham the following day.

> Down to Gehenna or up to the Throne,
> > (I told myself smugly)
> He travels the fastest that travels alone.

At three in the morning Brindle and Jack arrived and blasted their way into The Scholar Gipsy. The night porter, having woken me like a professional wrestler to check that it was indeed these for whom I had reserved a room, reluctantly admitted them. The next morning it snowed: no racing. Brindle appeared in the MCC tie. Since this time there could be no possible explanation I did not ask for it. Jack rang up some cronies, most of whom turned out to be Tipperary trainers or their 'associates', men of mean, shifty and unshaven countenance, and they all went off in a fleet of cars to a snooker hall in (of all places) Malmesbury. Brindle and

8

Jack returned alone in the early afternoon.

'Those effing Micks won all our effing cash,' Brindle said. 'Come on, Jack: kipping time.'

Five minutes later she appeared in my room, where I was resting with a book.

'Come on, soldier,' she said. 'Bloody Jack's passed out on me.'

'No room here,' I said.

'Double bed in our room. Bloody Jack goes out. You move it.'

She looked so determined, indeed murderous, that I went with her. When we reached her room, she pitched the swinish Jack on to the floor, removed her clothes and then mine with a rough but practised hand, and then engulfed me.

And very nice too. An ogress she might have been to look at, but she had the right touch and the right rhythms. Although I was, like her, six foot high, I could not compare in solidity, breadth or muscle; and she handled me kindly but brusquely, like a doll, picking me up from one patch of her anatomy and putting me down on another, indicating what was expected and giving tit for tat. All of which was lovely until it was seven o'clock.

'Dinner,' I said.

'We needn't bother with that,' said Brindle, who had been recruiting herself with draughts of neat whisky in the intervals of manipulating me. 'There's plenty of whisky and gin on the mantelshelf if you need a sharpener.'

I got firmly out of bed. So did Brindle. She took my clothes, which were piled by her own on the sofa, and locked them into the wardrobe. It was the only hotel wardrobe I have ever known the lock of which actually worked.

She threw the key out of the window, bounded back into bed, and took a colossal swig from the whisky bottle – not the one on the mantelshelf but the ancillary one under the pillow.

'Another round,' she said, reaching across the room for me like an octopus, then holding me above her as if I was an infant to whom she was about to give suck.

So we had another round. I could only just make it: Brindle went of like an H-bomb.

'Best yet,' she proclaimed; and then, by the mercy of God, begun to doze.

The wardrobe door wouldn't give an inch. How to dress for departure? Jack's clothes (in a pretty bad way) were still on Jack. Only one thing for it: the orange stockings (with garters, thank Beelzebub, not suspenders), the green check costume, the stiff collar with the MCC tie, the galumphing black brogues. But I should surely be spotted as male from my face and hair, and at once be shamingly arrested? *Ahhh!* Brindle's racing hat, which she hadn't yet worn as there hadn't been any racing, was sitting on the dressing table: a fabulously curtained, buttressed and domed construction of felt and feathers – enough to hide my head, my neck and much of my face, the rest of which was, in those days, smooth enough (in a freckly way) to pass as female.

The bedroom door was secured by some device that could be operated from inside without a key. A huge retch from Jack and a prolonged and bubbling snore from Brindle drowned the elephantine exit of Brindle's brogues. But how to get clean away from The Scholar Gipsy? There could be no question of paying my bill at the desk in this get-up. Steal Brindle's car? No key. But now, behold, a coin box, in dead ground from the foyer. Twopence in Brindle's side pocket. The taxi firm from which I had engaged and then cancelled a car for the races was delighted to oblige – 'Yes, sir, by the rear entrance, of course.' Some notes there were in Brindle's breast pocket, which she had somehow preserved from 'the effing Micks', not enough to hire the cab to London but easily enough to cruise into Oxford and take a train. My luggage? I must send for it later.

By the time I reached my club I had become used to Brindle's clothes, was indeed rather enjoying them, apart from the stiff collar; but residual caution intimated to me that it would be wise to enter the place by the ladies' annex, from which I could sneak through to the stairs and my bedroom (retained during my absence) where other clobber was left behind and waiting.

'And whom did you want ... madam?' the porter said.

'Captain Raven.'

'He's gone to Cheltenham, madam.'

'But I happen to know he'll be back early. Tonight.'

'At this hour, madam?'

'Very shortly. It's only half-past ten.'

'Very well, madam. If you're sure he'll be back, please wait in the anteroom.'

Good; I could get upstairs by the lift in the corridor behind it.

'Pray tell me, madam,' said a prim and aged member who was leaving the anteroom with his wife (Mrs. Grundy with knobs on) as I passed through, 'by what right or authority are you wearing an MCC tie?'

'A relic of my late husband,' I said. 'He was bashed in the balls – conked on the napper, I mean – by a beamer. For what business it is of yours,' I added, inspired by the garb and spirit of Brindle, 'he left me a cool one hundred and fifty grand and a very obstinate dose of the clap.'

And so to my room and safely to bed.

I sent The Sign of the Scholar Gipsy a cheque to pay for my room for the full four nights I had originally booked, and asked them to retrieve and return my clothes. They answered courteously that my clothes had been 'incinerated'

11

'By what right or authority are you wearing an MCC tie?'

when my guests had set fire to their wardrobe (having lost the key, they had seen no other way of opening it and fetching their own kit out), thereby causing damage of £337 13s 9d, for which they held me liable, to say nothing of Mr. and Mrs. Lofting's unpaid bill of £60. My present address, they respectfully noted, was Breedon Barracks, Shropshire: they would be very reluctant to have to trouble the Commandant in case of my continued default.

January 1, 1987, Penrith

My story was liberally applauded by most of the company at Vanushka's but not by General Pavey, who don't care at all for the notion of a commissioned officer of the Queen wafting about in drag.

'Not my fault,' I tell him. 'Pressure of circs.'

'Better go naked,' he snorts, 'naked and honest. Did you ever hear the story of Athamas Ainsworth of the Horse Gunners?'

'Please tell us, sir,' says James, as meek and sweet as a quirister. 'I hear your stories are famous.'

(Dear little Jamie wants to be allowed to drive the General's Bentley.)

'Well,' says the Brigadier-General: –

Brigadier-General Pavey's tale, Royal Military Academy at Woolwich (*circa* 1912)

Athamas Ainsworth was a GC* at Woolwich just before the Great War, always known as Windy Ainsworth because some bright johnnie found out that Athamas in the old days had been a son of Aeolus, the god of the winds, don't yer know. Now, Windy Ainsworth had one ambition under the moon – to put up the ball buttons of the Royal Horse Artillery when he was commissioned, which at the time of this story was getting pretty close. So to this end he worked liked a lascar, and played rugger (to get good character marks, though he'd much sooner have played raquets) like a whirling Dervish, and rode round and round the training ring till he and his nag were like a centaur, and generally carried on like some early Christian maniac who would have been fed to the lions for his faith – this, as I say, being that true salvation lay only with the King's Troop of the RHA, outside of which there was no life worth living.

So there you have him, d'ye see: Athamas Ainsworth the Enthusiast. But as the nickname of Windy may have suggested to you, there was another and more amiable side to the fellow. This side was occasionally visible at a piss-up after a rugger match or a band night, but the lads that really knew Windy said that there was one thing above all that really brought out the common humanity in him, and that was yer elder woman. Windy adored women old enough to be his granny or his great aunt – and they adored him back, as what proper woman wouldn't, a tall, spanking Gentleman Cadet in mess trousers as tight as the skin on his big round bottom.

* Gentlemen Cadet

14

And of course this little foible of Windy's was a blessing all round. Not only did it give a lot of pleasure to a regiment of females from the General's Lady to Mother O' Grady, it kept Windy, whose prick got good and stiff four times a day, carnally satisfied and out of any possible trouble. Women who are well past their half century know their place and don't want to change it; they don't get pregnant or hysterical or possessive or jealous or suddenly desirous of leaving for Cannes or Gretna Green in the small hours. They're just grateful for a bloody good bang, which they always had from G C Ainsworth, and then, while they heaved their bloomers up, it was ... 'Now off you go back to your books, Athamas dear', or 'Windy darling, or 'sweet young sorr', or 'naughty duckie', or 'thou horny little devil, thou', or whatever the case might be. 'You know very well' (or 'Ye ken muckle clear', etc. etc.) 'that your final examinations begin on Monday week.' So back to his desk went Windy, having taken the edge off for the next two hours or so and being now calm enough to pursue his essential studies in geometry and ballistics and military law and tactics and the rest of it until it was time to have it off with Toffee-Apple Kate on the bench of her kitchen, or the Farrier-Serjeant's mother-in-law in the Farrier-Serjeant's outside khazi, or the Dowager Lady Hitchkiss in the conservatory of The Glen.

All, then, was for the best in the best of all possible worlds (pleasure in streams and little risk of scandal or the pox) when Windy, having passed his exams *cum laude* and being all ready to march off the parade ground in three days' time with the Sword of Honour (a dead cert for appointment to the RHA), became acquainted with Bertha Brett, the Adjutant's wife's widowed aunt, next to whom he was seated at the Adjutant's private farewell dinner for cadet under officers of Windy's year. 'Big' Bertha Brett soon spotted

Windy's form, felt him up and down under the table from the soup to the savoury and whisked him off into the rhododendra while her niece entertained the company with an aria or two. And it was there in the rhododendra that Athamas discovered Big Bertha's erotic speciality: when she came, which was pretty quickly, instead of laughing or crying or howling or gibbering, Big Bertha used to fart – an enormous, rumbling, *de profundis* fart, which began quite modestly with her first twitch, mounted steadily to a thunderous blast during her many and awesome subsequent spasms, and subsided with a gurgle and a hint of a bubble during her valedictory vaginal shudder, the whole accompanied by a rather pleasing aroma of well-hung grouse.

So much did Windy and Big Bertha please each other that (taking advantage of the sycophantic encore that sounded from the drawing room) they decided to stay for another *parti*. Better even than the first. Windy guilefully slid in his beautifully curved sabre right up to its hilt; after thirty seconds the lady's thighs began to quiver and a breeze to sigh from the rippling rubber of her fundament; the quivering became a momentous heaving and threshing; the infant gale soughing from between her bounteous buttocks began to rend and to roar; and as Windy's heroic flood smashed through the dam, the lady gave three throbbing belly bulges, a final glutinous crutch wobble, and (as before) emitted an expiring anal gurgle which ended in a bit of a bubble ... a bubble rather longer, louder and more bubbly (Windy apprehended) than the time before. And another thing: the fragrance of grouse was more pungent. *Tout court*, ladies and gentlemen, Big Bertha had followed through.

Which might not have mattered so much, had it not been that the gallant Athamas had made of his tunic and overall trousers a cushion on the damp earth for the lady's tender *fesses*. And even that might not have mattered too much had not Athamas (ever hopeful of swift amatory encounter) omitted, earlier that evening, to don shirt or underclothes, an omission of course totally concealed by the tunic of the day, which reached half way down the thighs and was buttoned or clasped right up to the throat.

Thus a crisis in the career of Athamas Ainsworth, the peerless Gentleman Cadet of all his intake, was clearly at hand. He could vanish over the wall as he was – and would certainly be arrested when he reached the guard room on the way to his quarters. He could have borrowed some of the lady's scattered attire, but such a masquerade would not have seen him over the obstacles which he must encounter and was in any case unworthy of an accepted aspirant to the ball button of the Horse Gunners.

There was only one honourable way. Leaving Big Bertha still gasping in the aftermath of total orgasm, naked save for his mess Wellingtons (which reached becomingly half way up his well muscled but still hairless calves) he marched into the drawing room disdaining to conceal his slowly subsiding and glossy peego. The aria died on the Adjutant's lady's lips, which formed a pout of pleasure, swiftly displaced by an affectation of horror. Dead silence followed. Not a woman in the room that did not devour Athamas with her eyes even as she turned them bashfully aside.

'Mr. Ainsworth,' said the Adjutant at last, 'and pray, sir, what is the meaning of this?'

'Mrs. Brett and I were walking in the garden, sir, discussing her late husband's service in the Punjab, when Mrs. Brett was overcome by a most distressful enteric ague, so severe that it might even have been an internal haemorrhage. I had no choice but to assist her ... with such materials as were available to me ...' (Windy sketched with his hands the absent garments that should have concealed his magnificent nudity) '... that might alleviate her calamity and assist her

17

... a pout of pleasure, swiftly displaced by an affectation of horror

in her toilet. I am come to tell you to summon a doctor
without delay ... unless of course Mrs. Brett's long sojourn
in the Orient with the late Major Brett has rendered such
attacks frequent or habitual, and she is accustomed to recover
without assistance other than that of her relatives or her
servants.'

Or, in other words, 'I have been shafting the rorty old
bag in the bushes and she's gone and overdone it. If you want
to avoid a blazing scandal you will accept my explanation,

however implausible; you will not call the doctor but clear up the mess yourselves (her maid is probably expert by this time); and you will bind all present to silence on the ground that it would be invidious to broadcast the poor old biddy's sad state of debility and incontinence which has been caused (let us at least postulate) by long and loyal service with her husband in treacherous climates.'

The Adjutant pondered. His wife snitched another look at the Apolline Athamas, and nodded to her husband. Big Bertha was carried indoors (through the back way) by the domestics. Windy was accommodated with a suit of the Adjutant's; and a bowl of punch was served, over which all present gave assurance of their discretion.

It has been conjectured (added the General) that the newly commissioned Athamas paid his score to the Adjutant's lady before being ordered to his first posting with the Royal Horse Artillery and while the Adjutant himself was absent (a week or two later) at an annual field-firing exercise in Wales. The conjecture is true as allegory rather than as an instance of actual adultery; for, as Athamas once confided in me, 'She was a fine woman but too young for me by twenty years and more. However, we did manage to fudge up some kind of production with the ball-shaped silver stopper of one of her husband's hunting flasks.'

January 1, 1987, chez Vity and Vanushka
by Penrith

Immediately after dinner, Milesy Malbruges sets up Vity's backgammon set (at least he has had the good taste to leave his own set, which is so huge and professional as to be most damnably vulgar, in his car). Moustache undulating in anticipation, he invites challengers. Two step forward: myself (sheer perverse folly) and JBB (needs to recoup his losses on the caviar wager). In the end, Milesy chooses JBB: both of us are clearly sheep for the fleecing, but JBB looks so decent (with his snowy hair and his apple cheeks) that it is impossible that he should win, whereas I look just nasty enough to have a chance at long odds. Cunning Milesy takes the copper-bottomed option. Vanushka, looking anxious, hovers about a bit.

'Where's the doubling die?' says Milesy, fingering the accessories of Vity's set.

'It's got lost,' says Lucrezia Lippit, who is also hanging about.

'Lost? Whereabouts?'

'Someone left the board open on that low table,' says Lucrezia. 'Vity sat down for a zizz, but missed his usual chair (which had been moved) and sat down on the backgammon set instead. Now, Vity had a hole in his knicks. When he snored, the outgoing air set up an ingoing current through the hole and up his ring; and as luck would have it this current sucked the doubling die right up his jacksie. You remember, Vanushka?'

'Of course I remember. It was that evening I left the lobster mousse in the freezer and it came out like a sorbet. It's somewhere in Vity's viscera, that doubling die, Milesy.

You'll have to play for a set stake. No doubling this trip,' she says, jutting her jaw.

'Very well,' says Milesy the diplomatist. 'Shall we say a hundred?' he says to JBB. 'Usual penalties for a gammon and so on.'

'Usual penalties,' says JBB, whose face is all rumpled and goose-pimpled, like a crushed leg of cold guinea fowl.

They toss one die each to decide who gets first throw. Milesy has a 5, JBB a 1. Milesy makes to throw both his dice with his hands, but,

'No hand jobs here, Milesy,' says Vanushka. 'There's a perfectly good shaker – one for each of you. The shakers were too big to disappear up Vity's jacksie.'

So Milesy takes a shaker and shakes out 2/1.

'Two tits and a navel,' Lucrezia says.

Milesy moves one of his back markers three places; and then JBB throws a double 6; back markers out on to Milesy's bar and two down to his own bar from the corner five. Another 2/1 for Milesy, who covers the piece he moved first time.

'Somehow, Milesy, I don't think Jesus loves you very much,' says Lucrezia.

'Early days yet,' grates Milesy.

JBB throws double 4, then double 4 again (while Milesy throws like a pregnant netball mistress), then double 5, double 4, and then 4/5, thus taking off a single piece which Milesy has now left behind in JBB's ground and blocking him entirely from throwing on again. Milesy drumming fingers, not chuffed. To cut a longish story short, JBB then throws off without a hitch, and though Milesy has just managed to crawl on again, his piece is still in JBB's ground.

'Backgammoned, Milesy,' says Vanushka. 'Pay double for the gammon and double it again to make four times for the backgammon.'

21

'We agreed no doubling,' snarled Milesy.

'No doubling with the doubling die. But you yourself insisted on "usual penalties".'

'Only for the gammon.'

'You said, "Usual penalties for a gammon *and so on*." "And so on" just has to be the backgammon. What else could it be?'

'Right,' says Vanushka. 'What else could it be?'

'Under the international convention,' girds Milesy, 'the backgammon is no longer penalised.'

'I'll just settle for the gammon then,' says a radiant JBB.

'No you bloody well won't,' snaps Vanushka. 'The rules in Hoyle state that a backgammon is penalised by quadrupling the amount lost on the basic stake. Milesy knows that as well as he knows the colour of his own short hairs.'

'Hoyle has recently been emended,' blurts Milesy. 'The basic stake is only *trebled* for a backgammon.'

'That's not what it says in my edition,' insists Vanushka. 'You pay up according to the house edition of Hoyle, Milesy, or you go right out of the house. Now.'

'No chance of revenge?'

'Of course –' began chivalrous JBB.

'– No time for that,' says Vanushka. 'We've all got to play Trivial Pursuit. *Now*,' she barks like a regimental Serjeant-Major bringing a parade up before handing it over to the Adjutant, 'because if we don't start now Lucrezia will get pissed. She'll get pissed even if we do start now, but not *arseholes* pissed, so with any luck she won't knock half the house down with her car when she leaves and her driving seat will still be dry when she gets home.'

'Darling,' says Lucrezia to Vanushka.

'A piece of paper?' murmurs Milesy to JBB.

But old elephant ears Vanushka hears the cunning sod.

'No pieces of paper,' she pronounces, 'except bank notes.

Cash, Milesy. What've you done with that lot you won on Boxing Day? Come on, boy. Dig.'

Milesy digs. Vanushka examines each of the eight fifty quid notes before passing them on to JBB. I start telling the story of how my old chum Dick Brewer won the final of the annual championship at Brooks's, one grand in prize money and side bets he'd taken against himself for ten, in much the same way as JBB has just triumphed. The only difference was, says I, that Dickie was as drunk as a washerwoman and JBB isn't. 'With enough doubles,' I tell them all, 'you just schwamp – I mean, sramp – I mean, swamp your opponent.'

'Watch out *you* don't swamp something before the evening's out,' raps Vanushka. '*Trivial Pursuit*,' she proclaims. 'Bloody Vity's gone to sleep sitting on the goddamn set. Yank it out from under his knackers, Beatty – good girl. Now then, darlings. Lucrezia Lippit knows every fucking thing in the world which there is to know, and Beatty Belhampton is so sharp that she can cut through marble just by pissing on it, so it's really a match between them.'

'Beatty Belhampton,' brags Lucrezia, 'has as much chance of beating me at Trivial Pursuit as she has of going down on the Emperor of Japan.'

'Want to bet?' asks Beatty.

'Sure I wanna bet. I'll lay you five to one in twelve-inch vibrators, payable on demand, that you don't beat me at this evening's game of Trivial Pursuit.'

'Done,' cries Beatty.

All throw the die. First turn to Lucrezia. She lands on brown – Art and Lit.

'Who wrote *The Trial* and *The Castle*?' reads the question-master (Brigadier-General Pavey) from the first card in the stack.

'Fucking Kafka,' trills Lucrezia.

'Wrong,' says the General. 'Franz Kafka, it says on the

23

back of the card. I'd have accepted F. Kafka, but not the wrong Christian name. Next.'

Next is James. Lands on green for Geog.

'General Pavey,' proclaims Lucrezia, who has only just recovered enough to speak, 'is as sour as an old maid's dugs.'

'Mrs. Lippit,' remarks the General in a kindly tone, 'is unfortunate enough to be an American, and so does not understand about sportsmanship. James's question about Geography: what is the Gulf Stream?'

'A warm stream of salt water which crosses the Atlantic Ocean from Northern America to the British Isles, sir.'

'Warm stream of yellow piss,' says Lucrezia.

'Players that answer another player's question are fined one turn,' adjudicates the General. 'Five turns if they answer it wrongly, as is indubitably the case here. Next.'

Next is Beatty Belhampton. Lands on pink. Entertainment.

'Who was Laurel's partner in many films?' reads the General from the card.

'Hardy,' says Beatty as meek as a daisy.

'*You,*' squeals Lucrezia at the General, 'deliberately gave her an easy question.'

'It was the next card out of the stack.'

'The next card out of my vagina. *You* hope she's going to come to your room in the night and play banana fritters.'

'She won't want to bother with me,' argues the General, 'if she's got all those vibrators you wagered. *Ergo* it is in my interest to give her difficult questions – if I want to cheat, which I don't.'

The logic in this shuts Lucrezia up. She begins scooping liqueur choccies out of a flaunting Christmas box and hoovering them down in handfuls while waiting for her next turn – still four rounds away. Both JBB and I are boobing badly. Milesy fails to answer 'Who wrote Hamlet?' and

24

sneaks off to bed pursued by thin, malignant laughter. Vanushka lands on History Cake, remembers that Richard III is popularly held responsible for the strangling of the little princes in the Tower, and leads the field by one slice.

'Clitoris,' Lucrezia apostrophises to her hostess.

'With brass knobs on,' returns Vanushka.

And so the thing goes on. After her turns begin again, Lucrezia steadies up. No more risks. She gets Geog. Cake and Sports Cake, comes up level with Vanushka who has History Cake and Lit. Cake, but both are trailing Beatty, who has History Cake, Lit. Cake, Sports Cake and Geog. Cake, only needing two more slices to approach the centre and be asked the $64 question. JBB and I continue to boob. James modestly collects his slice of Entertainment Cake – some bloody pop girl. He throws on to Throw Again, throws on from there to Art. and Lit., tells us that R. L. Stevenson wrote *The Black Arrow*, throws on to green for Geog. Cake, collects with the pronouncement that Toronto is in Canada, hits Throw Again, hits Throw Again yet again, hits brown for Art and Lit. Cake, makes another slice by recalling that Milton wrote *Paradise Regained*, moves through all the other Cakes without stopping, throws to the centre, and pauses while the other players select the most poisonous question from the next card.

'This'll fuck him up,' says Lucrezia. 'Who was hidden among women on the island of Scyros to stop him being taken to the Trojan War?'

'Achilles,' says James primly. 'I'm reading Classics at Cambridge, you know.'

'Dear Christ,' says Lucrezia. 'I didn't know that anyone in the world still did that.'

'The fact remains,' says Beatty, 'that James has won and the game is now over. Since I was ahead of you at the close, you owe me five twelve-inch vibrators. What are you going to do about *them*?'

'Lesh play the game out,' burps Lucrezia.

'No,' comes judgment from the General. 'Unless agreed at the start otherwise, the game is over when one person has definitively won it, the remainder being placed in the order that then obtained. I hereby award Beatty Belhampton five twelve-inch vibrators, payable to her on demand by Lucrezia Lippit, in due accordance with the terms of the wager struck.'

'Okay,' pipes Beatty, 'so where are my five twelve-inch vibrators?'

'How do I find five fucking vibrators at this time of the night?' growls Lucrezia. 'Strain 'em out like turds? Give me time for Chrissake.'

'You said payable on demand. If Mistress Beatty now demands and you default,' rules the General like Rhadamanthos among the Dead, 'you must provide whatever alternative form of payment Mistress Beatty Belhampton may require of you.'

'Apollinaris,' crows Beatty, naming Lucrezia's prize Labrador.

'Apollinaris is worth two and a half grand in sterling money,' rumbles Lucrezia, 'and is not going to be given to some middle-aged flippertigibbet madam who writes runny crap for women's magazines.'

'So produce me five twelve-inch vibrators,' Beatty persists, 'on demand. *Id est*, darling (if you Yanquee's understand Latin), NOW.'

Lucrezia is on the fork and she knows it. Then a glint comes into her eye. 'Righty-oh,' she rasps: 'I'll be right back.' She tumbles out and within three minutes she tumbles back in. 'Come and look, everyone.'

The ingenious *savant* has pinched everyone's car keys from the silver plate in the hall where you leave them at Vity's in case your car has to be moved in a hurry in Vity's small

26

'Come and look, everyone'

drive. So there are five cars – Vity's, JBB's, the General's Bentley, Beatty's and Milesy's all with the engines turned on and the gear sticks juddering.

'There you are, and sod you rotten,' says Lucrezia to Beatty. 'Five twelve-inch vibrators. Which are you going to try first? I haven't started up my own little Morris 1000, because it's one of those old fashioned two foot gears – too long even for you.'

January 2, 1987, chez Vity and Vanushka
by Penrith

Bad start to the day. JBB a little 'liverish' ('Father's got a crapula') and can't eat more than four of Vanushka's lovely bangers. Then it's James's cue to sulk when the General sends a message by Beatty to announce that he will have his bangers in bed and not attend the meeting at Ayr, whither all of us are bound this day, so that puts the kybosh on J.'s hopes of piloting the Bentley.

'Unlike Pavey,' says Vity, 'failing to appear on parade.'

'He came to attention altogether too often last night,' Beatty tells us. 'I did try to stop him overdoing it but he kept on telling me some rhyme ... "Upon the heath there lives an old moke/Who very seldom gets a poke/And when he does he lets it soak." But surely he couldn't be thinking of himself? There must be plenty of girls quite happy to go

28

by-byes with the old darling. He's got bags of style and he's still very vigorous.'

'Yes,' says Vanushka, 'and exceedingly fertile with it. Or hadn't you heard?'

Beatty obviously hasn't.

'Then you must be the last female in the kingdom not to have. The very name of Pavey puts terror into the hearts of women years past the change. That's why he very seldom gets a prod. There are stories of matrons who've been cranked up again by the General and had children younger than their grandchildren. Clearly, Beatty, even you still have a lot to learn. I hope you wore your thing last night.'

Sullen silence. One more person for whom the day has started badly.

Before anyone can leave for Ayr, the huge stone gatepost, which Lucrezia, on leaving in her Morris 1000, has somehow propelled backwards and aslant the drive, has to be rolled back to its place (difficult, since it is a tetrahedron) and set upright. Butch Beatty's muscular shoulders and straining, nutcracker thighs (limber, too, from their recent application to the General), plus the inspiring leadership of the Major, bawling from the upstairs lavatory window, plus the languid assistance of JBB, James and myself at last do the trick.

January 2, 1987,
en route to Ayr

So here we are, off to Ayr Races. JBB, at the wheel, reminded that he owes a pony each to James and myself for the caviar bet and is unquestionably in funds after the Milesy Malbruges coup –

'– How would you like to treble your money?' says JBB to the pair of us.

Greed permeates the car.

'Quite easy,' JBB goes on. 'Lucrezia has asked the whole of Vanushka's house party to dinner tonight at the Labrador farm. But I'll lay you both 2 to 1 against our going. My money says we'll dine at home.'

'So if we *do* go to Lucrezia's according to plan,' says James, 'both the Raven and myself will collect seventy-five quid – twenty-five which we've won already and fifty more for the new bet.'

'That's right.'

'Know anything, do you? Like Lucrezia rang up to cancel while you were forcing down your bangers?'

'I swear not. I'm just your poor battered old father, trying to give you an amusing time.'

'All right, taken. Is the Raven on?'

'Yes,' says I. 'I'm on.'

'Always remembering,' says JBB, 'that if we do dine at home you both collect nothing?'

But James isn't listening as he's just spotted a security picket outside Willie Whitelaw's gate.

'Poor old Viscount Condom,' he giggles. 'What a terrible job they've landed him with.'

'What job?' says JBB, who sees little point in reading

news that doesn't concern cricket or racing, all of it being either silly, pathetic, mindless or just plain horrible.

'Yes, what job?' calls I, that share his view.

'AIDS,' James informs us breathily. 'He's preparing a report on how to stop it.'

'And how does one stop it?'

'One is chaste before marriage,' says James neutrally, 'and faithful to one's partner after it. Rather dull, I must say. Oh yes, and there is a suggestion that we might examine blacks before we let 'em through Heathrow, as Africa is heaving with it. But the blacks say that would be racist.'

'The thing is quite clear to me,' says JBB.

'Expound then.'

'This is the age of DIY — Do It Yourself. Need I say anything more? You don't catch anything nasty from masturbation, the company you keep is exclusive, and you can have fantasies to match the excesses of Tiberius.'

'Really, father,' says James, 'that is simply middle-aged cynicism. Besides, one is still thought to be more or less safe with girls.'

'Unless they've been playing Christmas crackers with bisexual boys, or used an infected needle to pump their dope in,' observes JBB, who turns out to have been into the matter more closely than one might have thought.

'One wouldn't know that kind of girl.'

'Wouldn't one? You know Hetta Sterling, who's ridden in every point-to-point that ever there was in our own dear county of Kent, and also rides regularly in NH meetings at Plumpton, Fontwell and Folkestone? Well, her dear little eighteen-year-old daughter was put inside for dope while you was off at Peterhouse last term — she'd been dishing it out to the other lovely students at her agricultural coll.'

'So one read, and thank you,' says James.

'*She* is just the sort of girl that *one* might have met,' says his father.

'But no one ever said she had AIDS. At least,' pronounces James, 'the upper class does use clean needles for its smackeroo.'

'But what about all those bisexual and infected boys she might have slept with?'

'Well, what about them? The truth is, father, that one is too young to be sold *Death* – by you or by the Government advertisements. One cannot spend the rest of one's life wanking. One must just use one's instincts in picking one's women. Anyway,' prescribes James, 'one always carries condoms. There's a new firm which is having them done in one's school colours. Club and regimental colours are to follow. Perhaps we can get General Pavey a 9th Lancer set? They say Jim Swanton's in a hell of a state because he can't bear to think of anybody sporting a rubber carrying the Arabs' colours. The Band of Brothers are a bit het up too –'

'– A light blue and black johnny would be rather pretty,' I speculate.

'The trouble is,' adjudicates James, 'that it might be confused with an Old Etonian one; or some dim girl might think one had a Cambridge Blue for something: and that,' he summed up rather priggishly, 'would be false pretences.'

In this vein we came to Ayr. A decent, level, handsome course, with excellent arrangements of a simple kind and pretty pleasant people (except those from Glasgow) in the enclosure. Nice setting too: only real snag is some blocks of breeding boxes down at the far end of the course.

January 2, 1987, Ayr racecourse

Milesy Malbruges is already there, guzzling yellow curry with Beatty Belhampton; Vity and Vanushka coming later. Milesy has had a tip but won't part with it for under a tenner.

'I had to pay Maxie two score,' he whines.

'Don't buy it,' says Beatty to us. 'I saw the slip – it's a piece of odds-on rubbish. Churchill Court it's called.'

'The Raven and I have put Churchill Court in our main yankee* with Coral,' remarks James.

'Put in something else instead.'

'Too late, darling,' I tell her. 'I phoned that yankee though to Coral's office before we left.'

'Well, ring up again and change it. Have you got Jennie Pat in that yankee?'

'No.'

'Well, ring up and put Jennie Pat in instead of Churchill Court.'

'They won't like it.'

'All right,' says Beatty, 'have the same yankee again, but with Jennie Pat instead of Churchill Court.'

'Why are you so keen on mucking our yankee about?'

'I've got a feeling in my bones.'

'In her vibrator,' mutters James to me. 'But you know, Jennie Pat *has* got a very decent chance.'

'Right you be,' I concede. 'Let us put Jennie Pat in an entirely new yankee with Churchill Court, as they're in different races, along with two more from the old bet – those at the longest odds.'

* A yankee is a bet featuring four horses in four separate races: it comprises all six double combinations, all four treble, and the four-horse accumulator. If the punter does the single bets as well, it is sometimes known as a 'yap'.

33

And so it was arranged.

*   *   *

'Did you know,' says Beatty, at the top of the stand just before the Jessie Pat race, 'that the sexiest things in the world are red-headed Scottish lads?'

'Who says so?'

She names a rather ponderous Scottish historian.

'On what evidence?'

'Having them. Apparently they come more fiercely than any other boys he's ever been with. With tumultuous cries of abandonment in Gaelic. The only trouble is that like all red-headed people they smell absolutely vile while they're doing it.'

Jennie Pat now wins like a brick. Two of the other horses in our Jennie Pat yankee are at other meetings, and come in (the board in the Tote Credit Office tells us) at 5 to 1 and 8 to 1 respectively. James does a rapid calculation.

'If Churchill Court comes in first,' he tells me, 'even if only at 3 to 1 on, we shall clear five hundred. A cool monkey.'

So here we all are in the stand again at the beginning of the Churchill Court race.

'I've had two monkeys,' says Milesy Melbruges, 'with Halbroke's man on the rails.'

'Then I hope your luck's changed since last night,' says JBB.

'What *is* the point,' says James, 'of putting on a thousand pounds to win four hundred less tax?' (Churchill Court is now showing at 5 to 2 on.)

'It's a dead cert,' says Milesy fatuously.

'You know damn well there's no such thing,' says James. 'Not but what one very much hopes that in this instance you are right.'

'Another thing about red-headed Scottish laddies,' says

34

Beatty. 'My informant says that their stuff is particularly good for the skin. You want to catch it, somehow, and rub it in immediately after.'

There is a long silence while all present ruminate about possible techniques for doing this.

'With cupped hands, I suppose,' says Vity.

'Or you could direct it from source on to whatever area of skin you wanted to rub it into,' suggests Vanushka. 'On to the face, for instance.'

'You might get an eyeful,' says Milesy. 'It stings like hell.'

'How do you know?' says Beatty.

'In my French set at school,' says Milesy, 'I sat next to someone called Petherton. One day he put his hand in my trouser pocket, turned it inside out, and cut it off.'

'Damned cheek,' said Vanushka. 'But I don't see what this has to do with getting an eyeful of –'

'– Ah. Petherton put his hand in my pocketless pocket. Right?'

'If you say so.'

'And I got a rise like the Tower of Pisa. But then Petherton, although it was very much him that had started the *parti*, suddenly looked shifty and shook his head. After the class he apologised, said that he had suddenly remembered something that bothered him, and suggested an assignation for later ... when he could explain to me, he said, all about his problem. So (since we were in different houses and had to be extra careful) we made a rendezvous for the following afternoon, well out of the usual way, right down the river in a little creek that Petherton knew about. Fine, just fine. You never saw a man come in such an extraordinary and wonderful way as Petherton. Quarts and quarts and quarts of it. And that wasn't all. It seemed that his nanny had got careless with a nappy pin and made a kind of second or subsidiary hole in his drainer just above the natural one. So

35

apart from Petherton's main stream, there was a vertical fountain of superfluous liquid spurting upward from his second outlet. (We were standing up, you see, as we all did in those days.) And as I was leaning forward to inspect this phenomenon more closely, the fountain went into a sudden surge and bang into my eye. Which is how I know that it stings. But that wasn't all I learned, that day and later.

'For before we parted we got on to Petherton's problem, what it was that had caused him to desist so suddenly the day before. *Not* the ancillary fountain, said Petherton, that just amused people; but the sheer amount that came out. All right on the bank of a creek down the river, but very difficult to deal with in more constricted or less private places without special preparation.

'"But at last I've found the answer," Petherton told me. "When one thinks one is going to have it off in confined circs – form rooms, cinemas, chapel and so on – circs in which it is absolutely necessary not to be too conspicuous, I always use one of those bladder things that old men wear at long dinners, in case they want to pee and can't get out. They're sewn into the trousers. Trouble was yesterday in French, I wasn't ready – wearing the wrong bags, bags without a bladder. I shan't make the same mistake again."

'"Where do you get 'em?" said I. "Rather embarrassin', givin' instructions to one's tailor?"

'"I pinched a couple of pairs of my dead grandfather's."

'"Did you?" said I. "I don't suppose he grudged 'em. But doesn't it rather spoil the feeling, having the neck of the thing clamped round your cock? And it's not much fun for whoever you're doin' it with, rubbing away on the tube of a bladder."

'"Ah," said Petherton. "I've had a zip fitted. So until I'm absolutely ready my cock is as free as a birdie and my chums get a perfectly good grip. And then, at the last second, I zip

36

it in – and whooooosh, into the bladder ..."

' "Ingenious. Who fitted the zip?"

' "Our handyman at home. I said it was something to do
with amateur theatricals. I had to fill the bladder with water,
I said, and attach the neck to a tube which would coil up
out of my trousers and make it look as if water were spurtin'
out of my navel. And for that I needed a zip. So a zip was
fitted. I think one day I may apply for a patent."

'As to that,' Milesy tells us, 'I never heard anything more
about a patent. But I did get a demonstration. Next French
lesson, Petherton gives me the wink, and we're off – usin'
each other's pocket holes without pockets, if you see what
I mean. No trouble for me when I came – I was no slouch
in those days, but a decent size in hankies hid any damage I
might do.'

'And Petherton?' says black Beatty.

'Something went wrong.'

'That zip. I suppose he did himself an injury?'

'Nothing so simple,' says Milesy.

'The bladder sprung a leak? The stopper fell out?'

'Oh, dear me, no. Nothing mechanical.'

'Tell, for Christ's sake.'

'When Petherton got back to his house, he had to drain
the bladder. Very strong on hygiene, Petherton was. He'd
done it several times before (he told me much later) and
expected no problems. But this time ... well, he went to the
house bogs and took the stopper out of the bottom of the
bladder, then squeezed it as he always did – and out came a
stream of blood. He'd got so excited about me, you see, that
somewhere in his works he'd had a haemorrhage or a bust
valve or whatever. And now, now that he saw the blood
and *knew*, he fainted. Some time later he was scraped off the
floor of the loo – they were all open in those days – by some
chums who knew his habits. One of 'em buried Petherton's

grandfather's trousers and the rest ferried him up to Matron and handed him over without explanation. Just said they'd found him slumped in the bogatry.

'No one ever found out what was the matter, because the haemorrhage had stopped and Petherton took jolly good care not to do anything that might start it up again. So Matron diagnosed overtiredness and bad feeding – that was during the war, d'ye see? – and put P. to bed and fed him wizard tucker for a week. After which he emerged to resume his normal activities – all, that was, except one. Poor Petherton: he's never dared to do it since, with or without bladders, not with boys nor with girls, nor even with Mrs. Palm and her five beautiful daughters.

'And then it was,' says Milesy, 'that I learned, first, that old men wear bladders at banquets, and secondly, that what you don't know can't hurt you. *Before* Petherton knew about that blood, he was as spry as a bluebottle, he told me. But the minute he saw it – flat as a corpse.'

And now the race begins and Churchill Court runs like that horse in *Black Beauty* that gets dragged off to the knacker. So I tell Beatty.

'Yes,' she giggles, 'you know what that horse was called? Ginger. Do you suppose ginger horses are as randy as ginger Scottish boys? Or that their stuff is good for the –'

'– Really, Beatty,' says Vanushka, 'sometimes you go too far. I don't mind what you say about Scottish boys, but I will *not* have you making tasteless jokes about horses.'

'Hear, hear,' says Vity. 'I won't put up with anyone who makes a fool out of a horse.'

'Dear Jesus,' says Beatty, as Vity and Vanushka flit away to the bar. 'If there's one thing *I* can't stand it's horse-worship.'

'I wish they'd take Churchill Court off to the knacker,' says James vengefully, 'never mind that Ginger.'

38

'Don't let Vity or Vanushka hear you, or they'll put you to sleep in the boot room.'

'But I ask you,' says James. 'An odds-on favourite flopping about like a love-sick cow.'

'Quite common,' says Milesy, with unexpected stoicism.

'But you said it was a dead cert.'

'So it was. But there's always an unknown factor. In this case, for example, it is quite possible that the horse's aesthetic or social sensibilities were disturbed by those breeding cubes down there. Or perhaps it didn't like the smell of the jockey. Or wanted to have a crap but was too prudish to do it in front of all these people. Or just didn't feel up to scratch. Any of these things could distract the deadest cert that ever there was. All I meant was that on the known form, given the distances, the weight and the going, Churchill Court was a mathematical certainty. Life, as you will soon discover, troubles itself very little with the known form.'

'Anyhow,' I console James, 'we've got a very nice treble and two doubles from the three that did win. Not too bad. Puts the old scribblers' account into better shape – nearly even. So let's not monkey with that any more and do cash for the rest of the meeting.'

'Doing cash', we discover that the minimum accepted by the Tote at Ayr is now £2. Although this has been the case for some time in England, the canny Scots have held out and insisted (very rightly) on a minimum of £1. But now the overweening greed of the Tote has conquered even here. 'High administrative costs,' they tell us, 'and the bigger our profit, the more goes into racing.' Well yes; if they make a profit. But, since different sections of the Tote, both cash and credit, deal in starting prices and not only on the pool system, they could catch a nasty cold if someone goes clear with a lucky accumulator. They've guarded against this, of course, by sticking a stopper of £100,000 per client per day

39

on all accumulating bets, as from May 1, 1982, up till when they offered *no limit*. Why did they change this? Prudence? A fluky win against them of a million or more? No matter: change it they did; but even at a limit of £100,000 *per capita per diem*, they *could* come unstuck. A pity that would be: their accommodation for credit clients is improving all round England (and Scotland), and they often have the sense, particularly in the Midlands and the North, to employ bouncers to heave out members of οἵ πόλλοι who would otherwise clutter the place up, sheltering from the rain or simply asserting their supposed right not to be excluded from anything. What is more, the Tote employs very pretty and very jolly ladies: something to suit all tastes. So long live the Tote.

Milesy is now observed being very strictly spoken to by the Halbroke's man. Milesy (*fiat justitia*) is giving as good as he gets. Come on, our goy Milesy.

All leave in good fettle. Vity and Vanushka have been given a free magnum of champers and have forgotten Beatty's invidious remarks about the equine species. Milesy seems quite cock-a-hoop after his discussion with the Halbroke's narg. J. and I are chuffed with our treble and a nice little win in cash in the last race. Things are going too well: disaster due.

January 2, 1987, chez Vity and Vanushka by Penrith

If not disaster, comes anyway a nasty setback. JBB was right. Lucrezia rings to cancel dinner the moment Vanushka arrives home. 'That's the fourth time that bloody cow has done this: gets as pissed as a piewoman here, then can't have us there.' So James and I lose £25 apiece when we might have made £75. Well – at least we haven't touched the money yet so we don't miss it too sorely.

Vanushka rises to the emergency with *flair*. A brilliant kedgeree of salmon. JBB, still mightily conceited at his expertise of divination and at saving £50 out of his 400, shakes the cayenne too heartily and jerks the top off. An orange pile of cayenne floods his kedgeree. 'Have another plate, John?' No, no, says JBB, this is fine, he dotes on red pepper. After two mouthfuls, his cheeks and chins heave, his white hair stands on end (like old Provost Sir J. T. S. of King's when reciting Sophocles to lovely fresh freshmen) and the subsequent sneeze puts out three candles and lands a superb blob of snotch bang in Beatty's cleavage.

'Bless you,' says General Pavey (now fully recovered, it seems, from last night's Egyptian PT). 'Did you ever hear the tale of Tilly Wenlock?'

'Please tell us, sir,' pleads James, who still hasn't given up all hope of a go at the Bentley.

'Well,' says the General: –

41

Brigadier-General Pavey's tale (*circa* 1920)

Little Tilly Slim, the chorus girl, married Waldo Axminster, by whom she had two sons and a daughter, all as pukka as a pace stick, then got widowed by the war (1917) and after a little felt lonely and decided to have Lolsey Wenlock for his 15th-century manor and the money. Poor old Lolsey only really wanted to be left in peace to go shooting every day, but in the end he married Tilly because she was so damned persistent – kept getting invited wherever he was, and coming up to the Butts every day and ruining Lolsey's aim with her nittering and nattering and nidging and finally her nagging, so that Lolsey gave in at last for the sake (as he thought) of tranquillity.

So now Tilly had got his manor and his money, d'ye see, and someone to sit opposite at dinner – and then suddenly, with the change of life, she got an itch for Lolsey's flesh. She'd never meant this to happen, and she knew it was the last thing that Lolsey was wanting or expecting, so she went off to London to have an affair. No good. Tried Snuffy Valence of the Galloping Grocers but couldn't stand his corset, then Ricky Marmoset of the Coldstream but was put off by a wart on his wanger, and then Jacko Condor of the Diplomatic, who would make her keep her stockings and suspenders on, like a French tart in a rude photo – and none of this was any good, and anyway it was Lolsey she really wanted, so back to Mortmain Manor to try to ignite whatever powder might still remain in *his* firing pan.

No good, of course. She showed him pictures and she gave him enemas and she notched him with a banderillo and frotted herself in front of him with a rhino tusk – no good at all. Until at last, just as she was giving up hope, Lolsey

... ruining Lolsey's aim with her nittering and nattering ...

did what JBB did just now. He spilt the cayenne all over his tucker, but in his case he also dropped the pot on the floor and bent down to fetch it up, sneezing all the while like Beelzebub. But the pot had rolled all the way down to Tilly's end of the table, so Lolsey, who was a persistent bugger when he started anything, crawled along to get it, still sneezing, saw Tilly's knees approaching and had an inspiration. Up with her skirt and out with her knees and in with his physog and sneeze, sneeze, sneeze like a Maxim Gun into Tilly's jackpot; then, 'Oh Lolsey, I never knew it could be as marvellous as this', and all that sort of rot.

Something to remember when you're a hundred (says the General) and yer pecker won't peck, d'ye see? No one's grumbled about mine yet, but even for me the time must be coming when I won't function and I'd be glad of a nose like Caesar's or the Duke's to play Sir Lancelot (tirrah, lirrah, thank you sirrah, cried the Lady of Shalott). Bad for the nose though, if you excite it with pepper too often. Like this cocaine stuff, it's no good for the membrane or the bridge. Brings it down as sure as the pox. But I'm told these surgeon johnnies will fit you a silver replacement, if you think it's worth it. In Lolsey's case, he didn't have to bother any more about it, because it so happened that he was just developing a cold and Tilly caught it in her game bag, which put her off for ever and ever, Amen. Can you imagine – having to take a handkerchief out in company to blow yer twot? Or sneezing suddenly out of yer quimeroo?

January 2, 1987, chez Vity and Vanushka by Penrith

After dinner, Milesy was hell's keen to take JBB (or anyone else) to the cleaner's at backgammon. JBB uneasy, because in all honour he owes Milesy a return match. But the General comes to the rescue: 'I am the senior man here, so you'll play a match with me, Master Milesy, if you please.'

'A hundred a point, General?' grins Milesy, who has found the doubling die (hidden in the box of liqueur choccies – luckily Lucrezia didn't gulp it down last night) while Vanushka was running up the kedgeree.

'Pounds or guineas, sir?' the General says.

'Guineas,' says Milesy, hoping to win that much more.

(Those that are not amused by backgammon should now skip to the end of this match. Those that do like the game might care to play it through on their own sets.)

So off they go. Both refuse their first throws, so the doubling die is already on 4 (400 guineas). Two throws later the General doubles (to 800) and Milesy not only accepts but 'beavers' (i.e. returns the double immediately it is offered and is allowed to retain control of the doubling die as a reward for temerity) to 1,600. The General is playing a back game, keeping two pieces behind in Milesy's ground, on to which Milesy is marching his own men round almost as swiftly and solidly as JBB did last night. But at last Milesy has to leave a blob and a gap. The General needs 3/5 and gets 2/5.

'Hard lines, General,' smirks Milesy, and throws his own dice. He particularly does not want 6/5, which will leave him with a gap and two blobs for the General to aim at. 6/5 Milesy gets.

'Hard lines, sir,' the General says, and throws 3/3, which takes off both Milesy's blobs. 'Very hard lines indeed. The doubling die's with you, of course, so it's not for me to say anything: but I'd certainly accept a sporting double to three thou. two hundred.'

'Would you indeed, General? Well now, you've got one,' says Milesy, who can never resist a challenge. In any case, he still has a very fair chance, as the General's board, on to which he must throw his pieces back, is pretty grotty. So over goes the doubling die at 32 to the General, who executes a smart "beaver" to 64 (6,400 guineas or £6,720). Milesy throws both his pieces back on. The General takes them both off with a double 1 and makes up four points in his own ground. Trouble for Milesy – who, however, throws both back on with a double 5. But then they're blocked, so he has to move two that are nearer home, leaving the General a much easier passage for his two back markers. A double 6 brings these right up two points from the General's home bar. Milesy will have to move fast. Double 4 – and he's away with *his* back markers. Milesy and the General now both have 5 pieces *outside* their ground, to be got on to before they can start throwing off. The General throws 2/1, not much help, though he gets two pieces in. Milesy grinds his teeth and throws 3/2 – better than the General but not much help either, and the General now has the throw. A strong double could settle it either way. Double 6 for the General; double 5 for Milesy; honour pretty well equal: both have all in their own ground and one piece off the board. 2/4 for the General; two more pieces off, so three off in all: average. Double 4 for Milesy; four more pieces off: five off altogether. Things look thin for the General – until he too throws a double 4; four more pieces off, which is seven off out of fifteen. 1/2 for Milesy; two pieces off, seven off altogether out of fifteen. Even stevens but the General has the dice in hand. He throws 2/3 – and gets only one more piece off as point 2 is now empty. Milesy throws double 6 – four more pieces off, eleven off out of fifteen, only four left on; if he throws a double of two or better next time he goes right out. The General now needs a double or he's had it (seven pieces left on and two more throws at best – he *must* get four off to stay in the game). He throws double 3: four off and only three pieces left on, but Milesy now to throw with four pieces left on, all of them on the 2 point. A double 2 or better will win for Milesy, but now; 2/3: two off and leaving two on the 2 point. If the General throws a double, getting all his three remaining pieces off, *he* has won; but he throws 6/4, enabling him to clear two off while one has to remain on. Milesy, in order to get his two pieces off the 2 point, can throw absolutely anything except a 1 and a something else, for if he does that the 'something else' will certainly take one piece off but the throw of 1 will carry the other piece only one point forward, where it must remain till Milesy's next throw — which he is not going to get. Milesy rattles the dice in the box, his teeth clicking and his moustache crackling: 6/1. The General *must* win: any old throw will take his one remaining piece off the board.

'Suppurating, syphilitic cunthooks,' Milesy says, but in quite a gentlemanly manner.

'I know how you feel, dear boy.'

'One more game, General?'

'I think not. The excitement is too much, at my age. But I'll tell you what, Master Milesy. When I was a subaltern, your dear father, Mavro, bailed me out with the bookies – I only owed a few hundred but that was a few hundred too much, and at any minute the pencillers were going to come banging on the barrack gate, and there an end of my career – except that your old dad bailed me out, as I say. He had his money back when my aunt Marigold died a few months

47

later; but I always felt I really owed him something more for the sheer fellowship of the thing. So I'll pay my debt to your old man now (and may the Devil let him rest) by letting you off this debt of yours to me, and may God or Satan make of you one hundredth the man that Mavro was – though I take leave to doubt the possibility.'

January 3, 1987, chez Beresford
by Penrith

Wretched morning. Damp, foggy, chill as the River Styx. Cancellation announced from Sedgefield, whither we thought we were bound en route to Stamford, for the night, and so home.

So it is decided to watch the four races which are being televised from one of the big southern meetings and leave afterward. Vanushka will put up a snack lunch. James and I propose a series of crackerjack bets, including a very heavy yankee that will make the layers scream with terror. I telephone these down to Sunderland, who politely consent to pay for the call and show no signs of screaming with terror.

How to get through the morning? I have brought a book – several. JBB works at an article for *The Sporting Life*. James watches morning television (may God have pity on him): a large studio is full of youth, much of it black, brown or yellow; the whites are the worst of the lot, having green and orange hair arrangements and looks on their faces composed variously of conceit, hatred, discontent, total ignorance of anything worth knowing, and massive self-righteousness. A succulent and saturnine ex-Member of Parliament encourages them to whinge about all the things they hanker for, haven't got and think they are entitled to. Inevitably, AIDS comes up – not something they hanker for, of course, but something they have a 'right' to be protected against. A sub-cretinous girl in a boiler suit says it's time that 'they' did something about that, it's all 'their' fault anyway, why couldn't 'they' have provided nice new needles for everyone to shoot his dope with instead of nasty blunt ones that had been infected by half the slags in Edinburgh or Brummagem. Loud applause. An Indian gets up and says that they haven't got AIDS in India because Indians are so pure and fastidious – and then adds that Central Africa is full of it because Africans behave like pigs. Abusive howls, quietened by the ex-MP, who has a distinct look of Baron Samedi that lends him considerable authority. The Baron surveys the grave-yard, then calls on a Ugandan student from the London School of Economics (when was he last in Uganda?) who tells the world that the official figure for AIDS in his country is .0001% of the population, and that that little is a legacy of colonial rule, having been left behind by district officers et al who abused their positions of privilege in order to seduce and infect nine-year-old girls. When this has been satisfactorily settled, the discussion shifts to sexism in sport, and it is suggested that from now on a Test Match XI, to avoid discrimination, should consist of five men, five women and one hermaphrodite. James now switches off and begins to construct another explosive yankee, which we later telephone to Tote Credit.

Meanwhile, the party is beginning to break up. The

General has risen at dawn to take a taxi for London and an aeroplane to the Bahamas; Milesy has simply sneaked away, none knows whither; and Beatty Belhampton is making frantic preparations to get on the road to Warwick, where she must attend some conference about magazine methods of advertisement for male make-up or sausage meat, she appears uncertain which. The trouble is that she cannot leave until Lucrezia Lippit has given her the promised telephone number of a man who has invented a new kind of dog food which produces fertility in bitches. Beatty is anxious to do a (highly paid) publicity piece for this, and can indeed claim that she once ran a successful campaign for a very similar product intended to promote sex appeal in Aberdeen Angus bulls, so that she must have a good chance of getting the assignment. However, nothing can be done until Lucrezia gives Beatty the name and number of the inventor, and Lucrezia, according to her fourteen-year-old daughter in her house at Kirby Stephen, cannot be woken. The only reason they know she's still alive (says the daughter) is that she honks out the phrase 'Cunt's Death' every ten minutes, though without waking up. What, we all speculate, can 'Cunt's Death' mean?

Vanushka postulates that it is a term to denote vaginal aspects of the change of life; but surely, James counters, although the change of life brings an end of fertility (except, apparently, in the luckless paramours of General Pavey) it often enhances concupiscence. Vity suggests that it means demise by sexual over-indulgence in the female. JBB looks up from his article to infer, rather similarly, a dose of the pox. Beatty is sure she has the answer, and quotes Sir Thomas Browne:–

... the sanguinary turmoil of the subcutaneous labyrinths

50

of the daughters of Lilith when conjured by lunar fluctuation.

In one word, says Beatty, 'Cunt's Death' means the curse. Perhaps, we allow, but what on earth has Sir T. Browne got to do with it? The use of the words 'sanguinary' (i.e. bloodstained or bloody) and 'labyrinths' (i.e. graveyard and, by extension, death) as a metaphor for woman's apparatus closely connect the notions of vaginal menstruation and mortality, Beatty contends. 'Lunar fluctuation' clinches the matter. Thus: the curse = a monthly process of horror in the vagina now turned graveyard = the death of the vagina = the death of the cunt (vernacular usage) = Cunt's Death. All of which is all very well, but what precisely, we ask ourselves, does the *usage of the term* indicate vis-à-vis Lucrezia's present situation? Has *she* got the curse? Or is she warming up for it? Is she thereby excusing her sloth – in neglecting to produce dinner last night and in failing to rise this morning? Or is she simply using the expression as an anathema to express her hatred and contempt of all and sundry, of God and his entire creation?

January 3, 1987, chez Vity and Vanushka by Penrith

The question is not answered, though Beatty's immediate problem is (most unsatisfactorily) solved, when Lucrezia

51

The party is indeed reduced

rings up at about half-past eleven to say (a) that she can't begin to remember the goddamned name and telephone number of the goddamned fairy who's invented this goddamned dog food that is supposed to make bitches horny, and anyway the whole thing has got to be a goddamned con; and (b) that she'll be coming to dine with Vanushka this very evening. One would have thought that after Lucrezia's treachery the previous day, Vanushka would have told her to go to the Devil for her dinner, but not a bit of it.

'Yes, Lucrezia darling,' she croons, 'you be here about eight o'clock.'

Why such forbearance?

Anyway, it's goodbye to Beatty who kisses *tout le monde* energetically and drives crossly off into the fog. The party is indeed reduced. Only JBB, James and I, and our two hosts. We begin to feel quite melancholy, until Vanushka produces reviving fish soup with some brisk white wine – and the first race to be shown on television comes on at 12.45.

In this race, for our two stiffish yankees, James and I want Rookery Nook or Shamshuddin. Rookery Nook trips over the second hurdle and Shamshuddin runs out because the jockey loses his head.

' "Cunt's Death",' says Vity. 'What can she mean?'

Then James has a brilliant theory.

'Third race on television,' he says. 'Number 13, Con's Depth. Do you suppose she's had a tip for Con's Depth, and has confused the name – or that her daughter had mistaken what she's saying –'

'– I wouldn't put it past her,' says Vanushka, 'dirty minded little slut –'

'– Or that she's just sounding odd in the early morning,' James goes on, 'and that all the time she's trying to remind herself, or to *tell us*, to back Con's Depth in the 1.45 this afternoon?'

JBB comes briefly out of his article.

'Con's Depth was brought for a thousand sovereigns as a yearling,' he tells us, 'failed more dismally than any known horse in the history of racing on the flat, his best performance being ninth out of eleven to Serpent's Lair in a seller at Folkestone, and proceeded to run (if possible) worse after being gelded. In the end he was put in for two hurdle races last season, in both of which he refused at the first hurdle. The 1.45 this afternoon is a three mile and two furlong chase; Con's Depth has never before tackled fences on a racecourse; he is being ridden by a moronic stable lad with a petty criminal record (shop-lifting jelly babies and exhibiting his tool to elderly Anglican nuns) who has only ridden in one steeplechase before this one, on which occasion one of his boots fell off. I do not really think that we can support Con's Depth.'

'Perhaps it's a tremendous job,' says James in an unconvinced way, 'and someone's told Lucrezia about it.'

'No harm in having a tiny bet each way,' I say, and go to the telephone, ring Tote Credit again, and have £2 each way at Tote Prices.

In the second race, the 1.15, we want Jagger's Twist or Lord Charlie for our yankee. Jagger's Twist goes in at 9 to 1, whoopee. So the position before the third race is as follows. One of our yankees, the one with Shamshuddin and Lord Charlie, is virtually dead as two horses have failed already; the best it can produce is one double. The other yankee, Rookery Nook (beaten), Jagger's Twist (first at 9 to 1), Come to Momma (in the next race) and Run Rabbit in the fourth is very much alive: for £30 (it is a £3 yankee) will be going up on Come to Momma, which should start at about 9 to 2, and so if Come to Momma should oblige we shall have a real heap going up on Run Rabbit for the treble and two more doubles. Other interests in the third race are George Washington, the third selection of the ailing yankee, not backed singly, liable to start at 7 to 4 and so of little import, and the joker, Con's Depth, which might or might not have been tipped by Lucrezia in her somnolent matutinal babble. This last is now showing in the betting at 66 to 1.

Off at 1.47. George Washington, to everyone's relief ('Such a boring selection,' says James, 'the sort of dreary horse that father might select in his dreariest mood') unshelves his rider at the first open ditch, while Come to Momma is running steadily at fourth or fifth of the seven runners, and Con's Depth is still a clear last if still just in touch. But the moronic delinquent who is riding him seems to have had a lesson or two: he is properly turned out in well fitting boots and has apparently established an easy relationship with his horse; if the jockey is not too demanding, one feels that Con's Depth will probably carry him past the post – no more than that, but even that was quite an improvement on previous performance.

Coming down the home straight for the first time – and there is a nasty accident. Two (fancied) horses interlock their rear legs and fall horribly at a plain fence, bringing down a third. Since George Washington is already gone, and there are seven runners, it leaves only three in the race: Come to Momma, now two lengths in the lead, Study Fag trailing him, and Con's Depth, well in the rear but still not absolutely out of touch.

'So,' says James, 'come on Come to Momma, please God, with thirty quid on your back. But Con's Depth could make a nice little consolation.'

'Con's Depth cannot win,' says JBB. 'If it does, I shall hang myself from a lavatory cistern.'

'All we want,' says James, 'is that little pig Study Fag out the way.'

'Better Study Fag than Con's Depth,' says JBB, 'if racing is not to be reduced to a farce.'

'Bravo the purist,' cries Vanushka.

'We're talking of money,' retorts James. 'Come on, Come to Momma ... Hang about, Con's Depth. Get lost, Study Fag.'

And suddenly, to our joy, with one mile still to run, Study Fag starts to go backwards.

'First time out at this distance,' concedes JBB. 'Come to Momma should do it ... though he drifted badly in the betting, from 4 to 1 to 7 to 1. I wonder why?'

The reason is now speedily apparent. After two miles Come to Momma has no heart for his task at all. Coming round the bend at the far end of the course, he idles like a curb-crawler and can barely be coaxed over the first in the home straight.

'I have the answer,' promulgates JBB, looking up from a huge black book. 'Come to Momma has never run on a left-hand course before.'

'I should have known,' says James crossly.

'He could still win for all that.'

Study Fag is flopping about like a barrage balloon on *terra firma*. Con's Depth passes him and forges slowly up behind Come to Momma.

'Consolation prize coming,' cackles James to his father.

'If Con's Depth wins,' says JBB, 'I shall leave all my money to a cat's home *before* hanging myself from the cistern.'

'Well, you can start getting ready to alter your will.'

For Con's Depth is now inching past the almost moribund Come to Momma, who simply stops dead when confronted by the next fence ... which Con's Depth manages to clamber over like an ass mating with a mare.

Con's Depth now has three fences to clear before the winning post. Study Fag, though still technically in the race, is so far behind that nothing can bring him back into contention ... unless, as seems all too likely, the now much debilitated Con's Depth falls or fails at one of the remaining fences. Heave-hoh and stagger, and he's clear of the third out. When he comes to the second out, he sort of eats his way through it.

'Only the last now ...'

Clump. Wobble. Out on the other side. Whoooops. The delinquent falls off but climbs on again. Con's Depth shambles past the post. About a month later Study Fag shags in, having made a full tally of the fences, a legitimate second.

'I'll go and get you some rope,' says James to his father. 'Please use the upstairs loo so that the downstairs one is still free for the rest of the audience.'

The screen flashes up the prices. It seems that Con's Depth started at 100 to 1 and will pay £871 – 30p to a pound stake on the Tote and £140 – 10p for a place. Over £2,000, that is, to refresh my Tote Credit Account. True, I'd smoothed it out a bit with yesterday's bets, but today's are beginning to bite, so that this win is real Mosaic manna in the wilderness.

'Stewards' enquiry,' flashes the set.

'*Shit,*' yells James, who has been promised a nice percentage out of my winnings to 'make up' for the disappointment about Come to Momma, 'what the Cunt's Death is that for?'

'Did you not observe,' modulates JBB, 'that that disgusting animal of yours absolutely *leaned* on Come to Momma just as he refused?'

'Come to Momma had more or less stopped already. He was right out of the thing and you know it. So what if Con's Depth did just brush up against him?'

'An irregularity. It might have affected Come to Momma's

57

power or will to jump. Now, Study Fag, on the other hand, committed no irregularity. They will give the race to Study Fag, just you see; so I shan't be needing that rope, though thank you for courteous service offered in the matter.'

And so it was. Con's Depth was disqualified outright presumably for 'reckless riding' by its jockey and consequent dangerous running and interference with Come to Momma, and Study Fag was awarded the race.

'If Study Fag had fallen,' enquires James, 'would they *then* have let Con's Depth have the race?'

'Oh, yes. The only horse still standing. But as it was,' says JBB, 'they had a decent chance to award the race elsewhere, and they, being purists like me, grabbed it. It really won't do, you know, winners paying over 800 to 1 on the Tote as Con's Depth would have done. It gets the sport a bad name – turns it into a lottery.'

'Rubbish,' says Vanushka. 'You know what still keeps us all going year after year? Despite the rain and the cold and the wretched food and the pompous know-nothing stewards and the bullying little men at the gate and the gross over-charging – like nearly a quid for a small bottle of soda? What keeps us going, in spite of all that shit, is the hope that one fine day a horse will pay 800 to 1 and *we'll have the ticket*. If every horse that won won on form or merit, think what a horrible bloody bore the whole affair would be.'

January 3, 1987, en route for Stamford

Having stayed for an early tea with Vitreus and Vanushka, and having calculated that the day's returns have effectively reversed (and worse) all the benefits that accrued to my account yesterday, we set off past Brougham Castle to join the A1 at Scotch Corner.

'No wonder Brougham was such a sullen brute,' says James, 'living in that heap.'

'It was in better repair then,' says JBB, 'and anyway he spent much of his time in Cannes.'

'But didn't he get ill of something,' I enquire of JBB (the historian), 'and have to come back here in the end?'

'He got sick of disappointment,' says JBB.

'Disappointment at what?'

'At finding out what a filthy crap heap the world was,' says JBB, 'viewed whether from Brougham or from Cannes.'

JBB has not done well on the day either.

We proceed glumly towards Scotch Corner.

'Everyone we have passed in the last ten minutes,' says James, 'looks as if he were either hellish inbred or even the product of incest. We might be driving through a country created by Hieronymus Bosch.'

James has found out about *him* at Cambridge.

'I assure you the people could be very much worse,' I console him. 'Try driving from Seville through south-east Spain; or spending a night at Missolonghi; or in Birmingham, come to that.'

In such mood we come to Scotch Corner.

'That place,' says James with venom, 'looks as if it is full of salesmen boasting about their Sierras and then going upstairs to shaft shopgirls.'

'You must have walked a mile or more in the night for the loo'

'Not shopgirls,' says JBB, 'nothing as wholesome as shop-girls; typists who call themselves secretaries. Their fee for being screwed.'

The cloud lifts a little as we drive down the A1.

'How did you get on in that bedroom of yours?' James asks me. 'You must have walked a mile or more in the night for the loo.'

'That depends on how often he had to pee,' says his father.

'I found a jug,' I enlighten them, 'and took it up with me to serve till the morning.'

'*Dis-gusting*,' says James, half in joke and half in prudery.

'Beatty caught me emptying it in the bathroom, but promised not to sneak if I gave her a go at my toothpaste. The trouble was, it was silver – some prize Vity had won for polo in the Army. It had been put in the kitchen in a special place for special cleaning. Being drunk, I didn't notice how grand it was, when I commandeered it, and thought it had just been dumped. When I came down with it, Vanushka was going frantic, wondering where it had gone.'

'How did you explain its absence?'

'I said I'd used it for drinking water. She knows I drink a lot of water in the night. "But it *leaks*," she said. "I know," I lied. "I put it outside on the windowsill." '

'A likely story,' says James.

'People should go back to using those beautiful china jerries,' opines JBB.

'We had them at my prep school. We used to watch each other pee,' I reminisce sentimentally, 'but there was *one* boy who would hold the pot right up against his stomach.'

'Mean hound.'

'He was punished. He tilted the thing so much that he spilt a lot on the floor. Matron smacked his bare bottom, and he got an erection.'

'So he wasn't really punished?'

'He was then sent down to the Headmaster to be beaten, and got an even bigger erection. The junior matron, who was a larky girl, told us later. She had to pour cold water on it, she said. But Belchamber – the boy – said that that didn't work, so she played with it instead until he had a very funny feeling and it went down.'

'Lucky old Belchamber. Just as I said, then: he wasn't punished.'

'His character was completely changed from that day on. He never stopped playing with himself or anyone else who wished to be played with.'

'Things weren't at all like that at my prep school,' JBB remarks wistfully.

'Nor at mine,' says James, 'though there was a gym mistress who made us all wriggle through her legs along the ground. "Scouting," she called it. If she liked you, she squatted right down almost on top of you. Sometimes she knelt instead.'

For some time all three of us considered this phenomenon in silence. Eventually,

'Did she wear tights or stockings?' I venture.

'Knee socks. She had blue veins on her thighs. Tell me,' says James, 'what happened about the leaking jug?'

'I went back to my room, and looked under the bed-table, where I'd kept it, and found, by the grace of God, that the boards were bare just there. A little damp but no damage. I threw lavender water on top, and that was that.'

'What did you do the second night?'

'I took a pint pot.'

'Was it big enough?'

'No. I had to empty it out of the window.'

'Could you *stop*? I mean, while you emptied it?'

'Don't be a pest,' says JBB to James.

'But one really wants to know. Since the Raven is being

so candid, one may as well take full advantage.'

'If you want to know, I went on – out of the window.'

'Then why didn't you simply do it out of the window in the first place?'

'It meant getting up on my toes, and even then I had quite a job to clear the sill.'

'Golly. The problems of you geriatrics.'

'It comes to us all,' rumbles JBB.

'Euthanasia is clearly the thing,' I observe.

'No, no, quite wrong,' James rebukes me. 'Remember Plato. We must stay at our posts, like soldiers, till our Commander relieves us.'

'He has a lot to answer for, that Commander,' comments JBB.

'Luckily,' I rejoice, as we nose into the car park of The George of Stamford, 'he provides consolations. Dinner here tonight will be one of them. The breakfasts are damn good too. You can eat three hot courses if you really concentrate, and take away enough fruit and cold meat for a week of picnics.'

Our reservation – three singles with baths – is in order. No nasty last-minute tricks by God (such as I have often experienced) on *that* account. Not this time.

'Thank heaven I'll be spared Father's snoring,' says James. 'At Vanushka's it was like the Zoo.'

January 3, 1987, The George of Stamford

At dinner spirits rise like a Zeppelin. Grilled baby lobsters and rare roast beef, with a Mersault and then a Chambertin, do much to make one more tolerant of Our Commander, however much He may have to answer for in other respects.

The first question that came up for discussion was, what would Milesy Malbruges have done if he'd beaten the General? Would he have taken the money?

'Obviously,' I opine, 'that's what Milesy's life is all about. He'd have won it fair and square. In fact he was very unlucky to have been beat.'

'But nearly £7,000,' says JBB. 'It's a monstrous amount to be playing for in a private house.'

'Vity and Vanushka are used to that kind of behaviour. And it's not as if the General were still wet behind the ears. He knows the rules as well as any man living.'

'Vanushka was very protective about Father,' put in James, 'but she didn't make the slightest effort to protect the General.'

'Yes,' I reply, 'because your father is as innocent as a tiny little cherub. But the General could take care of himself. No need to protect *him*.'

'I suppose not. Do you think he'd have paid up?'

'Oh yes. There was no cheating. Milesy is sharp, but he don't cheat . . . if only because he knows that no one would play with him if he did.'

'But,' says James, 'the idea of the old boy writing out a cheque to Milesy for 6,400 guineas is rather gruesome.'

'Men have gambled away a hundred times that.'

'Generals?'

'Generals, dukes, princes. They've run through whole estates in an evening.'

'Why do they do it?' asks James.

'At first because they enjoy it. Then to get their money back. First and last because they like being punished. Have you ever known a gambler do anything sensible with his money if he has a decent win? No. He just uses it to go on gambling. He wants to get hurt.'

'Why?'

'Guilt.'

'What's he guilty about?' James persists.

'Really, you're getting to be as big a bore as Socrates,' says JBB, 'like a walking catechism.'

'Only because one wants to know things which one does does not know. *What* are gamblers feeling so guilty about that they want to be punished?'

'They are feeling guilty about gambling,' I explain.

'But surely, if they never started gambling they could not feel guilty about it. What makes them start? It can't be desire to be punished for gambling if they have never yet gambled.'

'Agreed. They start because they are greedy and want more than they have, or because they are idle and want to pass the time, or, by extension, because they are bored and want some excitement. They know that they should not be greedy, idle or bored, and that there are pastimes far more worthwhile than gaming to be found without any difficulty. It follows that the reason they feel guilty is because they are so futile and shallow and trivial that they have chosen gambling.'

'So,' James challenges me, 'we are all three of us here futile and shallow and trivial?'

'I fear so, Socrates.'

'And we are also guilty because we are so, and because we took to gambling on that account, being too stupid or

65

frivolous for more serious pursuits; and all this being the case, we desire to punish ourselves by losing our substance at the gaming table?'

'So it would seem, Socrates.'

'The fact remains that we all enjoy ourselves hugely when we are winning and *not* being punished. How do you account for that?'

'We know that sooner or later punishment is inevitable – and that it will be all the more savage because we shall remember our present gains and hate ourselves for having lost them.'

'Yet although we know this, we make no attempt to put them by and save them?'

'On the contrary, we gamble the more heavily for our gains, on the one hand hoping to win yet more and, on the other hand, knowing that we shall, in the end, lose disastrously, however much we win first, and so attain to the punishment which we desire. The greater our present success, the more condign the punishment when it comes.'

'Has *no one* ever hung on to his winnings and given up gambling for good? Or perhaps gone on, but only playing for pennies?'

'Sarah, Duchess of Marlborough,' I observe, 'got out of the South Sea Bubble at the top, literally a few hours before it burst, and I think she was prudent thereafter. And Thackeray has a fictitious character, based on a real one, whom he calls the Marquess of Steyne, and who won a fortune gambling with his friends and never parted with a penny of it.'

'Horrible. Made a fortune out of his *friends?*'

'The character is said by some to be drawn from one of the royal dukes of the period, by others to have been taken from a lesser nobleman whose house was bankrupt and who used his wits to recuperate his capital. In either case the man, as you say, was horrible. And Sarah Duchess of Marlborough

66

was horrible – everyone was agreed about that. We conclude that gamblers that go on gambling are to be preferred to those that hoard their loot.'

A cheese soufflé arrives.

'Another beguiling gift from Our Commander,' says JBB, 'to make us put up with His ill manners and bullying.'

'Gift?' says I. 'We're paying £3 a head for it.'

'Gift in the broadest sense. Something which He, after all, made possible.'

'Along with famine and bilharzia. But while we're on the subject of *His* ill manners and bullying,' I remark, 'what did you make of Lucrezia's? Pretty damned imperious, I thought . . . cancelling her own dinner party at the last minute and leaving Vanushka up to the neck in shit, and then inviting herself *en princesse* for tonight?'

'I think Vanushka's used to it,' replies JBB.

'She certainly showed a very high degree of forbearance. Meek as parsley. "That's lovely, darling; be here at eight," or whatever she said.'

'What you have to remember,' JBB tells me, 'is that Vanushka loves her. It's just a simple as that.'

While I am digesting this, James puts another question:

'Do you think,' he says, 'that Con's Depth really was a tip she'd had?'

'That was your theory,' says his father.

'It could have been some kind of dream. Or she could have seen the horse in a list of runners somewhere and carried the name about in her subconscious.'

'Why that particular name?'

'Perhaps she had a brother or a lover called Con once upon a time. Or it could have been a girl she knew – though the horse was male. Con short for Connie or Constance?'

'More likely to have been a girl. What man's name does Con abbreviate?'

'There was a Kent amateur called Con Johnston. He was never called anything else as far as I know, but I imagine the Con was short for Constantine ... like the author of *When the Kissing Had to Stop*. Constantine FitzGibbon. Lucrezia is very literate: the name Constantine may have excited her – the first Roman Emperor to be converted to Christianity.'

'He was a real brute,' I tell him.

'Exciting, nevertheless. Visions and battles.'

'So you think the name Con's Depth got into her head and stayed there because of Constantine the Great, and that she just came out with it in her sleep?'

'What she came out with in her sleep,' says JBB, 'was Cunt's Death. Or so her daughter told us.'

Enter Milesy Malbruges.

'Staying the night,' he explains. 'Fundraising in the shires.'

'Fundraising for what?'

'Milesy Malbruges,' says Milesy Malbruges. 'I've just been dining at the Castle along the road.'

'Any good?'

'No. No investments for future events, and no cards or backgammon tonight. That's why I'm back so early. They're all sulking because Con's Depth was disqualified this afternoon. I'd tipped him, you see. And a bloody good tip too. Not my fault if the damned thing interfered with another horse. Mind if I join you?'

'Port all round,' says JBB.

'*Did* Con's Depth interfere with Come to Momma?' asks James. 'It didn't look much like it on telly.'

'I went to the course,' says Milesy. 'That's why I left Vanushka's in the middle of the night. And the answer is, no, Con's Depth did not actually interfere with Come to Momma; not through my glasses. And in any case any interference there might have been occurred at the fourth fence out and would not normally be taken into account.

68

But that daft lad Gemminy Quick, who was on top of Con's Depth, was talking to the other jockey. I could see that. And when he'd finished, Joey Sprott on Come to Momma went green … and Come to Momma loses her stride and stops dead. Story was on the course that the stewards had spotted Gemminy yakking at Sprott, and asked Sprott what Gemminy said.'

'And what was that?'

'"Joey Sprott is a screeny mother-fucker who's had twins by one of his sisters." Everyday sort of insult among boys like that, of course, though the fact that it put Joey off his stride for a single second probably means there's something in it. But the stewards weren't concerned with any of that: they just took a common-sense view that an insult which was, from their point of view, so appalling – criminal libel, if you come to think of it – must constitute foul play in running.'

'Would Come to Momma have stopped if Gemminy hadn't said his little bit?' I enquire.

'God knows. But even if he hadn't, Con's Depth would have beaten him. They've been working on this scheme for years. They've rigged Con's Depth to look like the mangiest dog that ever crawled along a gutter, and they've rigged Gemminy Quick to look like something out of a loony bin for syphilitic lepers. All the money was going on in betting shops all over Britain, in *tiny packets,* just before the off, so that the price wouldn't nosedive, and then what happens? Everything goes like clockwork but Gemminy goes and targets himself. He's been told, today is *it*, Gemminy, no antics, today you're born again and there's a whole thou. in it for you. But he can't resist dealing out a dish of the old Gemminy dirt, just for the hell of it.'

'It seems that Lucrezia Lippit got hold of that tip,' says JBB, 'or rather, she may have done. Did you give it to her?'

'Not I,' from Milesy, very firm. 'I wasn't telling anyone except my big steamers in the Castle – in case someone should have an honest wallop and bring the price right down. You see, my steamers have a certain delicacy in handling these matters, but some bluff old number like General Pavey, for example, if he'd got to hear of it, would just have tossed a couple of monkeys into the middle like two lead weights and screwed the whole operation to pieces.'

'If you told nobody, how did Lucrezia latch onto it?'

'Drink,' says Milesy, 'or so I've heard her claim in the past. You remember that story of D. H. Lawrence's, "The Rocking Horse Winner"? Boy rocks on his horse and the name of the winner just comes to him. Same kind of thing with Lucrezia – or so she says. If she drinks enough and goes on drinking, at last the name of a horse comes into her head though sometimes not until she's sleeping it off.'

'But this time ... if that *is* what happened ... it went wrong,' says JBB. 'For her, and for you too, Milesy – though you didn't get the tip out of a bottle. Who primed you, Milesy?'

'God or the Devil,' says Milesy, a bit madly. 'It comes to the same thing in the end. The Devil, you see, can only perform – can only get information and pass it on to chaps like me – if God wills that he should do so. Like that business in the Garden of Eden: the Devil succeeded in sneaking into the Garden *only* with God's knowledge and connivance.'

'One more item in the case against God,' says JBB to me.

'But not for the first time,' Milesy was saying, 'God conned the Devil. He only showed him Con's Depth first past the post, *not* the subsequent disqualification. A typical God-trick. But it's no good giving *that* out as an excuse at the Castle.'

Milesy muses.

'But mind you,' he says, after a while, 'quite often God's

70

pretty straight. For example. That skite from Halbroke's, yesterday, at Ayr. You saw him narging at me?'

'Yes. And we saw you narging back.'

'God told me how to settle that. He'd rung up the office in London, that skite, and found out that my account's a month overdue. "How dare you trick me into taking a bet for a thousand," he said, "when you've been owing us since November?" Come on, God, I think: give me the words. "You should have known the position," I told him, "before you took the bet. It's no good ringing up *after* the race." "I wouldn't have taken it if I'd rung up before," he said. "We reserve the right to refuse, or cancel, any wager if the account's more than two weeks in arrears without a special arrangement. Which in your case you have not got." "All right; go on and cancel the bloody bet," I said. "It suits me fine." "You can't get away with it just like that." Something in his tone tells me he's weakening. Now I wonder why that should be, God, I'm thinking. Can it be he's afraid of the edge in my voice? Well, no harm in trying a bit more of it. "So," I ask him, "why the bloody hell didn't you ring up *before*?" Really good and fine and fierce I'm getting. A very queer look comes into his face, very suddenly. I'd found the key. "Come," I say, "out with it."

'He mutters and mumbles and then starts his confession (for confession, as you will soon see, it is). He'd gone for a strain in the strainer (says he), a visit to the toilet, as he calls it, and when he's finished he finds all the loo paper's gone ("the personal hygiene tissue," he calls that), and it takes him five minutes to screw himself up to using his new silk hanky which his wife has given him as a New Year's present. And by then it's too late to be ringing up London about my *bona fides*. "Why are you telling me this?" I ask. "People don't usually confide like this in professional clients." He'd suddenly *flipped*, you see. One minute he'd been putting me

71

'"Why are you telling me this?" I ask'

down like a riding master bawling out a rookie, and now here he was, writhing and groising about and making intimate statements about silk handkerchieves. And then I knew what God (or the Devil) wanted me to do. Clearly this man got a high (so God told me) out of being humiliated. So:

"You dirty little swine," I say, "you are getting a *thrill* out of telling me what you did with that silk hanky. And what did you do with it *next*? Flush the whole fifteen guineas'-worth down the tube?" "No, oh no," he cries, "my wife would never forgive me. It is here in my macintosh pocket. It's such hell, I had to tell somebody. I must get it home, you see, and have it washed before tomorrow, before my wife asks why I'm not wearing it in my breast pocket." "You cancel that thousand quid bet of mine," I tell him, "which you should never have taken if you was doing your job properly instead of hanging around in public lavatories, and you agree to make no more beastly hassle about my account, or I'll be ringing up your wife to tell her to look in your macintosh pocket the second you get home. I know your beastly name because it's on the board under Halbroke, and I know where to find a telephone book."

'This was all bluff of course, it would have been a ghastly job going through the ten thousand Cohens in the directory and trying to sort out this one. What's more, he knew it was a bluff, but that didn't matter, d'you see, as long as I was giving him a good tough screwing, as long as I was playing his game with him.

'"Oh, yes sir, yes sir," he wails, as if he were going to bang his nut on the rails in a frenzy of homage, "oh yes, thank you, sir, just as you say, sir, and thank you so much for letting me off."

'So you see what happened,' Milesy diagnoses in The George of Stamford. 'God gave me the luck to start coming it grand, and the insight to see how this poor wretch was reacting. He wants to be felled to the ground and jumped on, d'you see, used as a doormat. He may even have made the whole story up, and used it to get me going as soon as he spotted I was the type he needed to rub his nose in the shit, real or imaginary. Or possibly it was all quite true, in which case ten to one he tells his wife the minute he gets home and begs her to birch him with the broom stick she rides to her coven on (for the wife of that sort of man just has to be a witch). Anyway, that's that: no more trouble from *him*, now or ever. Though of course Mr. Big in the head office may take a different view; in which case I shall have to call on God to help me to defend myself against him – to remind him that if his course representative on the rails has let me off, then let off I do be.'

'Well,' says JBB, 'since God (or the Devil) provides, on your theory, for the faithful, and since money itself is of no more account than Scotch mist, would you or would you not have taken the General's money, had you beaten him at backgammon? Would you have accepted this huge sum from your father's old friend, after a mere casual game in a corner of a friend's drawing room, or would you have let him off, in the spirit in which he let you off, and just said that money was merely so much paper and would come again when wanted, from your steamers or wherever?'

'Nice question,' concedes Milesy. 'Of course I'd have taken the old boy's money. He won't have much use for it, not much longer. He'd probably have wanted me to have it, to judge from what he was saying about my old pater. And as for the circumstances of the game, I say that where money is won or from whom is quite beside the point as long as there's fair play and both parties are willing … which was entirely the case here. Another thing; whatever a fellow may say about trusting in God or the Devil to provide, God and the Devil insist on *his* putting *himself* about a bit as well. After all, a fellow must keep going and the General's money would have been just what a fellow needed.'

'But as it is, you've got to hang around your steamers in the Castle? Are God and the Devil going to help you in that quarter? And how are you going to help yourself?'

'What it comes down to is this,' Milesy promulgates. 'If

74

a fellow just hangs around long enough, keeping his eyes open and without losing hope, sooner or later something agreeable is going to happen ... as it would have happened to me if I'd beaten the jolly old General.'

'Or to you and your friends, to say nothing of James and the Raven, if Con's Depth hadn't been disqualified. But neither of these things happened.'

'No,' Milesy admits. 'But something else nice will happen sooner or later, to you and to me and to everybody. Just you hang around and see.'

'When you refer to God' – this from James – 'do you mean God the Creator of the Universe, or your own personal daemon or genius? Such a personal daemon as Socrates had – or thought he had – who was always calling him to order when he started to get slack or tried to oil his way out of some obligation.'

'Hadn't really thought. A bit of both, I suppose.'

'And the Devil? Do you mean Lucifer himself, or one of his understrappers?'

'Surely they're all under His personal direction, so it comes to much the same. Just as I imagine my daemon – if I have one – is under the direction of God. Let it be how it will, so long as they let me jog along somehow.'

'One more question. Does your daemon confine itself to advice about matters of contingency? Or does it occasionally raise or issue a moral imperative?'

'What, like "Don't overdo the brandy", that kind of a thing?'

'That's sheer self-interest. One meant, rather, things like "Don't take green boys for a ride at backgammon, even if they do show willing to come to the table and the play's fair when they get there." Or, "Don't take it out on some wretched little Jew bookmaker, even if he is longing for you to tread on him."'

75

'Then a pox on moral imperatives. I've told you: he started the thing by taking it out on me; and God put me wise how to get the better of him.'

'God *or* the Devil, Milesy,' pronounces James. 'I think you should start to distinguish.'

'Look 'ee here,' comes back Milesy. 'You're just too young to start lecturing a fellow and upsetting him in his ways. I've been in the game twenty years, and I can't change now. But I have got one defence to enter.'

'Go ahead.'

'I am a punter. I put up my money and take risks, at racing or backgammon or roulette or whatever. I am *not* an exploiter, like the bookies, who shave the odds until they virtually cannot lose, or those casino johnnies, who let other chaps drain each other's blood at Chemmy while they take a percentage of the turnover. *Those* are worse than pimps: they are providing, on substantial commission, facilities for the meanest vice of all.'

'Gambling?' says James. 'The meanest vice of all?'

'Yes,' asserts Milesy. 'Trying to take another chap's cash off him without giving anything for it.'

'Come,' says I. 'What one gives him is a chance to take one's own cash off oneself. Not too bad a contract.'

'I still know it's mean,' insists Milesy. And to James, 'So there's your moral imperative.'

'Which you don't seem to heed.'

'I just enjoy gambling too much,' Milesy moans. 'So there's an end of that.'

'And so do we all enjoy it,' says JBB, 'and we've just had two splendid days of it, and had a lot of fun, and nearly won a packet, some of us, and none of us come quite unstuck.'

'Not quite,' mutter Milesy and I, 'not yet.'

'So,' says JBB, 'let's drink to our hosts, Vity and Vanushka –'

76

'– Vity and Vanushka,' from all –

'– And to great days and jolly days past, present and to come, and to the Big Win, the Six Figure Win, that we believe is waiting for all of us.'

'That's it,' booms Milesy. 'The Big Win that's waiting for all of us if we only hang around long enough.'

'Amen,' call James and I. 'Amen.'

'And so now, in bumpers, gentlemen ...'

'... To the Big Win,' we all chant, 'and a pox on moral imperatives.'

Twelfth Night, 1987, Walmer

Visit of Colonel O. 'Parafit' Paradore due this evening.

Rather uncertain what O.'s form will be. In the old days, when he left our regiment to join some parachuting mob, he was as keen as vinegar on things like fitness, alertness, man-management, thrust, keenness, example, etc., etc. His great desire was to be what he rather absurdly called 'Parafit', a concept which rolled all these attributes into one. By the time he'd broken his bones three times parachuting, and failed the Staff College Exam (though near top of the list) on a technicality, and been bombed in a whoreshop in Cyprus, and served under a teetotal and totally deranged CO in Borneo, things had started to change a bit. A long period in Singapore did little for his moral or physical fibre, and a long period up the Persian Gulf did even less. By then he was retired from the Army and working in a Vice-Consulate or some such thing, and 'Parafitness' had dropped below the horizon and almost out of memory. Still, I hear he's kept his shooting up, though very puffy, they all say, when walking up hills. Well, we shall see what we shall see this evening.

January 7, 1987, Walmer

O.'s visit a great pleasure for me and utter disaster for O. He put up at The Black Horse, where we had a decent enough dinner. Then gin rummy and Marc de Bourgoyne, which he'd brought from London as a special treat for me, but seemed determined to suck down the lot himself before he went back.

And sure enough, after the first two large glasses he started to be somewhat less than Parafit. Until then he was leading quite nicely; but half way through the third quintuple he began to miss his chances, and by the beginning of the fifth he'd just been blitzed and snided to the tune of £250, or not far off. So despite my protests he trebled the stake – and this time loses nearly a thou.

'Pay you next time,' he says. Fair enough; one can't take a cool grand off a pissed ex-comrade.

'Drive you home,' he says.

'Taxi will do me very well, O.'

'*Drive you home.*' The Marc de Bourgoyne will not be denied.

So drive me he does, and not badly, all things considered, and anyhow not a peeler in sight. Only trouble is, he's slammed his bedroom door (self-locking) on his key, and then shut himself out of The Black Horse, where they don't have a night porter.

When I rang him up in the morning, he'd spent the night in the back of his heap in the municipal car park, and been nobbled by the warden, who woke him up at 6.30 and charged him a tenner for using the place all night. He couldn't get into The Black Horse till 7.30, but he'd had breakfast by the time I telephoned and seemed quite perky.

'Pay you that thou. the next time,' he said, 'or win it back.'

So I asked him to dine in London, open date, whenever he cared to take the invitation up. No point in pressing the thing. My club, I told him; bearable spot of dinner and a beautiful backgammon room.

'Just the job,' he said. 'My luck may change at back-gammon. Do they have Marc de Bourgoyne in your club?'

'Yes, O. They have it.'

'I'll let you know,' he chirrups. And rang off.

One thing: unless he gets the better of his little weakness for Marc de Bourgoyne, his backgammon will be about as 'Parafit' as his gin rummy.

January 8, 1987, Walmer

Tailpiece to O.'s visit. He rang from London this am. He'd stopped for lunch on his way back to London yesterday, stopped much too long, and was breathalysed in Rochester, way over any licit limit. Spent three hours in the slammer before permitted to go on his way.

Poor O. One thou. light at gin, night in the car park, ten quid lighter for the privilege. And now this. He needs a bit of help from his daemon, as James would say.

January 10, 1987, Walmer

When I remember O.'s bustling prime (and my own, come to that) in Germany and Kenya, the thought of the luckless and squalid outing he's just been enjoying down here makes me feel a little sad. In this dead season of the year I recall the same season in the foothills of the Harz Mountains, thirty-three years ago, when it did not seem dead at all, because every day one had such a lot to look forward to (including the daily orgasm, however achieved).

There was, for example, the battalion boxing match against one of those heavy Welsh regiments, in Paderborn. I was boxing officer for the 99th Light Infantry in those days, and in charge of the party. You could have struck me

dead when the first thing their boxing officer (a great big
butch major, who was trying to conceal his ranker origins
under a sort of blustering *bonhomie*) said to me almost before
we were out of our three tonner was,

'Into the gym for weighing 'em, what? Easiest if we do
'em naked.'

So we did 'em naked, both teams.

Paderborn (January 1955)

I was rather proud of my shy, creamy, country boys, with
their nicely proportioned limbs, golden down here and there,
and classical, uncircumcised cocks. They might have been
out of a Boucher. The Welshmen, on the other hand, were
quite hideous. Either short, sharp and runty daws; or grinning moronic ogres, slouching and stooping, hair all down
their spines; or, in the middle weights, chunky hewers and
drawers with knotted calves, mean, fibrous thighs, and heads
like leering corbels. Their officer i/c boxing looked our lot
carefully over, with an interest neither sensual nor sexual,
simply in assessment of their possibilities in the ring. Then
he smiled at the prospect ahead, as well he might. It was
clear that the game was all up before it began. My soft-
spoken teenaged National Servicemen from Hereford or
Ludlow or (transferred from other regiments) from Somerset
or Cornwall had no chance at all against these Welsh bruisers,
mostly regular soldiers of well over twenty and so with an

extra two years (over my boys) of muscular development and malignant instruction.

Only one hope we had: most of my boxers were tall and slim and would have the reach over the stunted dwellers of the black valleys. Well, yes, the reach, perhaps, but little power behind it and little will to apply it.

To cut a tiresome story short, the 99th were indeed licked, but not as badly as I had feared. Intelligent boxing in the lower weights, use of agility and height in the middleweights kept our score well above the level of disgrace. Only in the light-heavy and heavyweights were we slaughtered. Although the Welsh do not produce many big men, when they do they produce monsters of bone, gristle and sinew; and all we could find to match these monsters was a lackadaisical and long-limbed tympanist from the band who had volunteered for the trip mainly in order to accompany one of his mates, a pretty little bugler who was fighting at flyweight (they were known as the spider and the fly), and a gallant serjeant of anti-tank guns who was cast like a barrel, huge and hard on the outside but full of slopping beer within, and so with a very vulnerable stomach for this fight. Still, as I say, apart from the spider and the barrel, both of whom were carried out of the ring early in the second round, we put up quite a creditable show, losing by three bouts.

Having thanked and congratulated my amiable boxers, and confirmed that neither the spider nor the barrel was in danger of anything worse than a crapula the next morning (this at their own expense, as the Welsh entertainment was sparse), I went to the Officers' Mess for a late supper. Here I was boarded by the ex-ranker Welsh boxing officer, who was clearly about to offer me slabs of unsolicited advice, which I, as a subaltern being addressed by a field officer from another regiment who was also my host must listen to whether I would or no. Earlier in the evening, as I have said, he was distinguished by a kind of coaxing bluster: now, secure of victory and in well-oiled, patronising mood, he assumed an air of inverted class condescension, as if to say, 'I am the salt of the earth and it is very good of me to pay attention to an over-educated and spoiled little ninny who has not the knowledge nor the guts (for his sort never have) to do a proper soldier-like job in this area or any other.'

'How long have you been boxing officer for your battalion?' he said.

'Six weeks.'

'You've been on a course?'

'I learnt to box at school. I understood how to score a bout and, at a need, to act as referee in the ring.'

'Not enough.'

'I dare say. I did not ask to be made boxing officer.'

At this stage O. Paradore (then a captain and not yet gone whoring after parachutes) came into the Mess. It turned out that he had been sent from our battalion in the Harz, late that afternoon, to attend an emergency conference in Paderborn about the representation of BAOR in the pentathlon at Camberley later in the year.

'Good evening,' said O. to the Welsh Major. 'I am O. Paradore of the 99th Light Infantry. I have been billeted on you for tonight and tomorrow night, as I must attend the pentathlon conference at divisional HQ.' And then to me, 'If only the brutes had told me about the conference earlier, I could have got here in time to watch your boys box. How did they get on?'

'Not too badly,' I said.

'Very badly,' said the Major. 'They were unfit, under-trained, without enthusiasm, and terrified lest someone should spoil their lovely looks.'

O. stared at the man, produced his glasses, and put them very deliberately on to the bridge of his scimitar-nose.

'You didn't tell me your name,' he said.

'Major Hopkins, of the Royal Welsh Borderers. In this regiment, I should tell you, field officers are addressed as "sir" by officers below field rank.'

'Not in our mob,' said O. 'Not in the Mess. Nor nowhere else neither, if it comes to that.'

' "When in Rome," ' said the Major, who had been friendly in his distasteful fashion when alone with me but had clearly been inspired with great loathing by the appearance and demeanour of O. Paradore, ' "do as Rome does." '

He seemed very pleased with this cultural snippet. I wondered if he had any more on offer.

'We are not in Rome,' said O. 'We are in a bloody horrible Kraut town called Paderborn. If we did as the Paderbornians do, we should be sodomising our wives and feeling up our daughters. What's all this about Raven's boxers being unfit, undertrained and the rest of it?'

'As I have just said. And without any enthusiasm or spirit.'

'Ah,' said O. 'Do you know why our team came?' he said. 'Simply to oblige. You are brigaded with us, and you Welsh enjoy a boxing match, and so when you requested us to send a team we did. Poor Raven here was at his wit's end. A keen new CO has told us to get boxing going again in our battalion – as you may know, we really specialise in fencing, of which I myself am in charge.'

'Interesting,' scoffed the Major. '*We* do quite a bit of fencing with bayonet and rifle – a proper man's sport.'

'As to that,' said O., 'we had the kit, the dummy rifles and the padded masks, but I ordered the whole beastly lot to be burnt. Foil, sabre and epée, that's *our* spree. But this is to digress. As I was saying, a keen new CO wants us to have a bit of boxing, and so poor old Raven was put on to getting it up, a few weeks back, just as all our older men were being demobbed and whole lot of green recruits were coming in from the West Country. And then you ask for a match, and the new CO says "Jolly good show – a splendid way to begin, Raven, a match with a comrade battalion in the same brigade", and poor bloody Raven has to look over rows of smiling and never shaven faces and decide whom to bring here to fight your squad of veteran gladiators.'

'Excuses,' said the Major. 'Not very good losers, are you?'

'We're good enough losers,' said O., 'when we're not sneered at. Now, you made a classical reference just now, to Rome. So of course you know about the Athenians. They were amateurs, like us of the 99th. They enjoyed their games but didn't make laborious and boring drill out of them. They came off pretty well at Corinth and the Isthmus and Delphi – you'll know all about that with your interest in the classical world – but were always beaten by the heavy mobs, the pros from Sparta and Acarnania, the musclemen, the pot-hunters. There was a poet called Pindar. You'll have read him, of course?'

'No, I haven't,' said the Major through clenched teeth. The man was getting restive. But O. had him in a corner, between a grotesque trophy for rugby on a ledge which projected sharply from the wall and the Mess grandfather clock, presented by some long defunct princeling, which effectively blocked his other flank. He could not move without damaging one of these exhibits, or making a frontal charge at O. 'No, I haven't read this bloody poet, Pindar,' he growled. 'Why should I have done?'

'Because if chaps start spouting their classical knowledge and talking about Rome, one expects them to be able to keep their end up in that line – unless of course they're just quacking philistine yobboes trying to show off. So Pindar, let me remind you, Hopkins, was a writer of lyrical odes in which he praised the victors in the Greek games at Olympia and so forth. And sometimes had a good word for the

85

'No, I haven't read this bloody poet, Pindar'

losers. Pindar said that gracefulness in boxing or wrestling or discus-throwing or chariot-driving or any of the rest of it was like pure water running over sand, but that brute strength without style was ordure and piss. And that when ordure and piss got into the running water, the water was turned into a sewer – that is, the sport in question was brutalised by hulks and bullies. Now, I didn't see the fighting tonight, but I had a word with young Lamb of our bugles on my way to the Mess here, and he pointed out your heavyweight going off duty. And I'd say that if you put a thing like that in the ring, you really have shat in the pure water of boxing (which, as we all know, can be a very pretty sport) and reduced it to poisonous slime. So now off you go, Hopkins, and report me to all the world from the GOC downward for insolence and conduct unbecoming and all the rest of the abracadabra, and the best of Celtic luck.'

'One of the things I learnt during fifteen years in the ranks,' said Major Hopkins, 'was never to bear tales of what was said or done by my comrades when off duty. I am not, you will find, a common sneak.'

Nor was he.

The Harz Mountains, the Mess of the 99th Light Infantry (Spring 1955)

'The pentathlon,' announced O., passing the decanter of Armagnac, 'comprehends the five following exercises: the Sabre, the Pistol, Natation, Equitation, and the Marathon.'

'Does it indeed?' I said, filling my glass. (All this was at a time when 'delicious drinks' were still a commonplace on the Paradore scene.)

'The idea is, you see, that you are escaping from a castle in, let us say, these very mountains. First of all you fight a sabre duel with your captor, an unspeakable Hun. Then you take the pistols off his cadaver, plunge into the moat, swim across it while holding the pistols above your head to keep your powder dry, shoot your way into the local cavalry barracks in order to steal the Colonel's prize charger, and ride away through the forest like Hades with all the enemy's secret and diabolical plans stuffed into the seat of your breeches.'

'And where does the marathon come in?' I said, filling

again and passing the decanter back.

'The prize charger falls dead beneath you ten leagues short of the frontier, and you have to do the rest on foot.'

'In riding boots, I suppose? And did you hold them too above your head in the moat, or did you wear them for swimming in? And what about the ink on the diabolical plans? Was it waterproof? Or did you stuff them right up your fund –'

'– Don't be tiresome, old bean,' said O. 'That's only a fanciful bit of theory, to get people interested.'

'Just a *teeny* bit old-fashioned?'

'In the championship itself,' O. went grinding on, 'as currently conducted in the British Army and as confirmed at the conference in Paderborn which I attended a few weeks ago, you are required to fight the best of nine hits with the sabre, shoot fifteen rounds at ten yards' range at a standard target with a competition pistol, swim ten lengths of the Aldershot Baths, ride six miles over the point-to-point course near Camberley (five-and-a-half circuits), and run twenty-five miles over Chobham Common.'

'Why are you telling me all this, O.?' I said.

'The truth is, old bean, that the battalion has to field ten men for this year's pentathlon. The Colonel says that at least three of them must be officers. So I've decided that you can come along as last string.'

'How generous of you. I might – I just might – have other arrangements.'

'If so, you'll have to go and explain them to the Colonel and probably to the Brigadier as well. The Brigadier,' said O. Paradore, 'is very keen that the Brigade should be well represented in the annual pentathlon.'

'So how can I help? With a lot of luck I shall hit the pistol target – once. If I don't drown in the baths I shall certainly break my neck on the steeplechase course (or vice versa). As for running twenty-five miles over Chobham Common, you know as well as I do that I should be sick, or have diarrhoea – or both, and probably at the same time – before I had gone two hundred yards. Really, O., has God or the Devil removed what's left of your wits?'

'Far from it, old bean,' said O. Paradore. 'You see, I have a plan, a brilliant, brilliant plan, which will bring high repute to both of us, in the eyes of our new and keen Colonel and our prestige-hungry Brigadier – even, perhaps, in those of the General himself. Now you, Lieutenant Raven, need a bit of high repute in those quarters just now. After that fiasco with your anti-tank guns ... leaving not just one but two of them behind on Luneburg Heath after the autumn manoeuvres. And not remembering them for three whole days.'

'No need to be spiteful. We got them back eventually.'

'Nevertheless, a little atonement might be tactful.'

'All right,' I snapped, 'what is this brilliant plan of yours?'

'You'll see, as it unfolds. In your elaboration of possible calamities just now,' said O. Paradore, passing the Armagnac, 'you forgot to mention the sabre. My whole plan turns on the sabre ... which, you should bear in mind, will be the first leg of the contest.'

Aldershot (Spring 1955)

While I was a wretched swordsman, I knew a bit more about fencing with a sabre than about anything else on the agenda. Captain O. Paradore himself had sometimes condescended to instruct me. The great thing was, when being instructed by O., to keep your sword arm covered by your hilt, as he very much enjoyed ripping the unwrapped button of his sabre right up one's forearm – practice with O. being in shirtsleeves and unmasked, in order to accommodate some fantasy of his about being Zorro or the Count of Monte-cristo. So one thing I had learned to do was to take up the correct position to protect my sword arm. And this, according to O., was all I had to do during my sabre bout on the opening day of the pentathlon.

'Just keep a proper guard, old bean, and Uncle O. will do the rest. Now, off you go for Queen and Country.'

As it happened, I had drawn a very skilled opponent – the BAOR champion with sabre and epée for the previous year. No question of it, he was going to make his five hits (best of nine) in less time than it would take the umpire to count them off his fingers. It was all going to be quite shaming, but what could a fellow do? Guilefully chatted up by O. Paradore, persuaded that this ridiculous caper was demanded of me by distantly lowering Colonels and Brigadiers, into whose good graces I should never enter again unless I submitted to such chastening – what could I do except maintain my guard as instructed by O. and see what he and the gods were preparing for me?

So there I stood while the D'Artagnan of BAOR flounced up, made a foppish feint, and then (had the thing been for real) carved my left shoulder off.

And there I still stood while the jackanapes lunged down my navel (so to speak) and out the other side, split my windpipe, sliced the top off my skull as if it had been a pineapple, and made a conic section of my nose as neat as the tertiary pox. Five hits to Cyrano de Bergerac. Call it a day.

'Well done, old bean,' cried O., as I came off the floor of the gymnasium, 'very well done indeed. You played it just as I hoped you would. Beautiful, that guard of yours, quite beautiful. You must be very proud of yourself.'

'About as proud of myself as if I'd produced a wet fart at luncheon in Buckingham Palace.'

'Don't be such a silly, despondent bean. And now go and have a nice rest. Swimming tomorrow, remember?'

'But *look*. You said you had a cunning plan that depended on the sabre and the fact that it was the first event. Well, I've been through it, and done just what you said I was to do, and ended up looking like a right c——'

'– "Come unto these yellow sands",' intoned O. unctuously, ' "And there join hands." I'll have no naughty words at the pentathlon. Simply do what you are told, O bean of little faith, and all will be resolved.'

The next day I was fished out of the baths with a hook after one-and-a-half lengths. The day after I scored two outers and an arc-lamp with my fifteen pistol shots. The day after that I was contemptuously deposited on the top of the first fence by a very thoroughly gelded gelding who fancied no further exercise under me. And on the last day, having run just over four hundred yards on Chobham Common, I duly started to be sick and was lucky to have discharged the last squirt of that job just in time to get my knickers down for the other.

'Oh well done, my bean, my darling bean,' carolled O.

91

I was contemptuously deposited on the top of the first fence

after each successive humiliation. 'You have exceeded my maddest hopes.'

'What the hell are you talking about?' I said after my grand finale, pulling my shorts up with a snap. 'I was promised high repute. You had a plan which –'

'– Yes, yes, dear bean,' sighed O. Paradore. 'I did indeed have a plan, which did indeed depend on your demeanour during the sabre fight and on the fact (bruited several times between us) that this was the first event of the whole circus. And as I planned, so it has come to pass.' He glinted at me through his glasses as if I had been a crystal ball. 'After your performance with the sabre on the first day, the umpires took me on one side (as I had hoped) and required of me, as your Captain, to explain what such an imbecile (athletically speaking) was doing in my team. Or would your accomplishment, they enquired, perhaps prove more glittering in other events? Oh no, I said: the sabre was the acme of your Pentathlonic achievement. Then why, asked the umpires, why oh why were you here at Aldershot competing?

'Because you had set your heart on it, I told them. You were the godson of captain Mungo Raleigh –'

'– I was no such thing –'

'– Please, dear bean. You were the godson of Mungo Raleigh, who won the thing (that at least is true) in the 'twenties. You yearned to follow in your godfather's footsteps, or at least to tread some small part of the way he had trodden. You ached to strive, though you knew that you could never conquer. And so, I told them, you have striven and strained, you have totally extended and totally exhausted yourself in order to attain to some kind of proficiency in skills that could never be yours – indeed so long and hard have you laboured to master what little you could (witness, for example, the perfection of your guard with the sabre) that I had not the heart to leave you out of my team.'

'You really have tricked me out as Grocko the all-time clown.'

'Not a bit of it, dearest bean. You must realise that *your* views are alien to most military men. Unlike you, *they* admire futile exertion: they call it "guts". So much do they admire it that your name will appear, at the bottom of the list, indeed, but with a special commendation for courage and endeavour. Won't the Colonel be pleased? To say nothing of the Brigadier, and possibly even the General?'

'What's in all this for you?' I said, knowing and nasty.

'Satisfaction that a friend and comrade has proved himself at last.'

'Come clean, O.'

'Well, the umpires are rather impressed by the great

93

trouble I've obviously taken with you, by the sympathy and encouragement I've lavished on you, and with my marvellous patience in such trying circumstances. A letter to this effect will be going to the Colonel. To say nothing of the Brigadier and possibly even the General.'

The Harz Mountains
(March/April 1955)

'Darcy Halberd's goin' away to be married,' said O. Paradore a few days after we came back from the Pentathlon. 'I've got to take charge of his cross country team when they go up for the twelve-mile steeplechase on the ranges at Höhne. Want to come?'

'Any tricks here?' I said. 'Any nasty little chores that I might just get landed with? Like walking the entire course to inspect the obstacles? Or sitting out in the rain, in the middle of the Höhne Marshes, to check the runners past?'

'No chores; cross my heart.'

'Well then. Have I got to be polite to a whole phalanx of rumbling redcoats? All those bossing brutes in charge of the thing and in charge of the other teams?'

'Even you,' said O., 'can, I suppose, be civil to your colleagues from other units? Don't keep looking this gift horse in the mouth. I'm offering you a trip of three days to Höhne, three days away from this battalion and its demanding new career-crazy CO; three days away from compulsory officers' PT at reveille every morning. Do you want to come or not?'

'Here am I: take me.'

'Very well,' said O., 'and thank you for your gracious consent. Now: tonight is Darcy's farewell ding-dong. He leaves for England tomorrow afternoon, and *we* leave for Höhne tomorrow morning, tomorrow morning at five-thirty, to be precise, so don't go getting arseholes drunk at the party.'

'Why do we have to leave so early?' I whined.

'Yours not to question why. In fact we have to be there in time for me and the team to walk the course in the evening.'

'I'm glad you're clear that it's *you* and the team.'

'You,' said O., 'will be checking the team's accommodation and our own, and making returns of the number of meals required, at Echelon HQ.'

'I can find no fault with that. I am fully prepared to undertake a minimum of essential duties.'

'Good of you,' said O. 'See you at Darcy's party. That German girl, Lorca, the NAAFI manageress, will be there. She's looking for an English husband, so watch your step.'

'I thought she fancied Darcy?'

'She did. But as you may have gathered he's going home to marry somebody else. She'll be watching out for a transfer – at a very high fee.'

Darcy's pre-marital party was taking place in the Alte Kröne, a respected restaurant which granted us long credit in return for occasional, dirt-cheap deliveries of NAAFI spirits, orange juice, cocoa, loo paper and other delicacies at that time scarce in the Fourth Reich, or whatever the wretched country called itself in 1955. What everyone has forgotten now is that at this time, though the Germans were about to become our allies or may even (officially and in theory) already have become so, the British Army was still in practice an occupying force and behaved as such. The proprietor of the Alte Kröne could not risk our displeasure, and neither could Lorca, the German manageress of the NAAFI up at our barracks, employed there as a guinea pig to determine the feasibility of future Anglo/German co-operation at that level. So far Lorca had been a huge success: flaxen hair, dreamy, nordic features, thrilling Hitler Youth bosom and buttocks, lovely long legs that went round and round you for ever – or at least went round and round Darcy Halberd for ever, no one else yet having been allowed even a lick at this lovely truffle, though Garry Strap, a bandy and pustular National Service ensign, claimed to have come against her hip, clean through his No. 1 dress trousers, while dancing with her at some jamboree over the previous Christmas. Anyway, Garry Strap was of no account with or without his No. 1 dress trousers, and Darcy Halberd was going on leave to be married, so who would now succeed to Lorca's favours and what about the 'transfer fee' which O. had been quacking about? It was rumoured that the price which she had originally demanded of Darcy was engagement, and that she had surrendered without it only because of her Teutonic frenzy for Darcy's Apolline face and Apolline limbs. None of the rest of us in the Mess had any such attributes (though God knows, had Lorca been inclined towards the Other Ranks, which she emphatically was not, she could have done herself very nicely among my beautiful boxers) and it remained to be seen what inducements this Rhine Maiden would require in lieu.

All of which brings us back to the cellar of the Alte Kröne, where, when I arrived, Lorca was dancing lasciviously with O. to the tune (played on the Mess hand-winding gramophone, commandeered for the occasion) of 'I've Got You Under my Skin'. Darcy himself was doing good work supervising the arrangement of the buffet, but suspended the operation for a while to take me into a dark corner.

'Now look,' Darcy said. 'Would you like the clue to Lorca? One of the clues, that is: the most important.'

'No.'

'I've *got* you under my foreskin,' sang O., sweeping past us with Lorca.

'Jesus Christ,' said Darcy. 'Look, darling,' he said (for though indisputably the most masculine member of the Mess he called all of us 'darling' to annoy the new CO), 'you're being very prudent, darling, not wanting the clue to Lorca, because that girl is simply a vampire. She'll either have marriage, or every drop of blood in your body, or both.'

'You seem to have a few drops left.'

'I've been lucky. You know why?'

'They do say your SA was so volcanic that she couldn't resist the eruption.'

'It wasn't just that. I discovered a little secret. This clue I'm talking about. She gets turned on by Heine.'

'By whom?'

'By Heine. The German lyric poet. She's quite an educated girl, you know.'

'So. By telling me that, you *have* given me the clue. The very last thing I want.'

'Don't worry, darling, you can't use it. You don't understand or speak German. But somebody that does only has to read her a few lines from one of Heine's lyrics, and she starts writhing around like a cobra. It's something to do with early sexual associations, she once explained to me. Her favourite mistress at school used to feel her up rather expertly while they read Heine together, and now she's stuck with it. Now then, darling: although *you* can't read Heine to her,

97

you can pass on the tip to somebody that could. And here's an elegant pocket edition. Get the wheeze? Heine starts her up at any place and at any time, so if you found the right reader you could, you just could, arrange rather a jolly little finale to this party.'

'Does she only go for the chap who's actually doing the reading? Or for anyone who's around?'

'That,' said Darcy, 'will be interesting to discover.'

I sat myself down at the buffet with a nice pint of hock and some foie gras, and started to consider two possible plans. Plan A: arrange an *exhibition* on the dancefloor. Plan B: arrange an exhibition on the dancefloor but muster the troops in such a manner that it had every chance of turning into an orgy. Plan B, of course. Now: who was to give the vital reading of Heine that would conjure the whole lark up? O. could do a bit of Kraut, but I certainly wasn't going to have his hairy body bared to spoil everyone's evening. Nor was I going to hand the key to Lorca's keep to that little rat Strap (who had done German for School Cert.), having seen him in the showers a few days before; not only was he bandy, but he had dhobi's itch and a horrid little prick like the tip of a wild asparagus. Hughie Long was the most delectable subaltern, with soft, gangly legs and a lovely fourth form grin, but then Hughie was a Baptist or something of the sort, and would presumably decline. Dick Cock would certainly *not* decline, but he was 'ginge' and had spots on his back. Richard Ivory, the randy Harrovian, could not read German. Finally I fixed on David Harrison, fresh out from OCTU, and before that of my own school, where he had read modern languages and been known (so a young cousin had assured me) as 'Fizzer' Harrison, because he hissed like a Catherine wheel the whole time he was doing it and went off at the end with a single enormous bang.

'Fizzer,' I said to him a little later.

98

'I hate that name.'

'David ... the high honour of the evening has fallen to you.'

I produced the pocket Heine.

'At about midnight,' I said, 'the gramophone will start playing a record of "These Foolish Things". At this stage you will come up to Fräulein Lorca, who will be having a drink at the bar, and start reading from this book your favourite lyric of Heine.'

'Why should I do anything so ridiculous?'

'Because you're being told to,' I snapped. 'If you want a pleasant time with this battalion, and don't want to find yourself doing orderly officer for the next two months on end (and don't think I can't fix that), you will fall in with a good-humoured request. Here is the book. You may find that you are rewarded beyond expectation.'

'I don't need a prompt. I've got half Heine's poems by heart.'

'So much the better. Remember: about midnight: "These Foolish Things": she'll be drinking with me at the bar.'

I hoped, you see (despite my misgivings about Lorca), that a residual benefit of the spell would spill over on to me.

So. Ten to midnight. The new CO arrives, invited (as courtesy on Darcy's part required) and having refused (as custom in such cases dictated).

'My wife Harriet came out from England to join me in my quarters this afternoon,' says the new CO, excusing and explaining his presence, 'and saw your invitation on the mantel. She was so eager to come that I had to bring her.'

Enter now, just behind him, one of those bossing, busy-bodying frumps that held the Empire together for a century and have been unemployable ever since.

'Captain Halberd,' she says, as if she expects him to curtsy, 'you leave us tomorrow, I understand, but you will soon be back with your beautiful bride. Where are you going for your honeymoon?'

'We are going for our wedding trip to Venice,' says Darcy.

A great 'Hump' from the frump. She resents Darcy's correction of the middle-class term 'honeymoon', I think. But that she hasn't even noticed. She's on about something else.

'Scotland, now, is so much more healthy,' she booms.

'Venice is booked.'

'May I know which hotel?'

'The Daniele.'

'Much too expensive for a young couple at the beginning of their career. You should change your booking to St. Andrew's. I have a cousin who runs a modest boarding house, with bed, breakfast and high tea.'

Darcy opens his mouth, but what he was to say we shall never know, because at this moment Dick Cock (as instructed) puts 'These Foolish Things' on the gramophone. The CO, who has the sense to see that his wife must be silenced, eases her on to the dancefloor. David 'Fizzer' Harrison approaches me and Lorca at the bar. I shake my head desperately. The CO's arrival has killed my plans dead. But Fizzer just glints. Of course he don't know what's up with Lorca, but he sees I'm now urgent to stop it – so he goes right on with it in order to spite me, remembering (who shall blame him?) the nasty tone I took with him earlier.

So out it comes. I give an English translation for the benefit of the good reader:

> Sweet comes April, sweet comes spring:
> Maidens dancing in a ring,
> While all the lusty boys do sing:
>   'Come with me a blue-belling.
>   A blue-belling, a blue-belling.'

100

'*Himmel!*' shouts Lorca, and begins to shake. She punches Fizzer in the face, catches me a great slap over the chops, butts O. in the chest, kicks Hughie Long on the kneecap, rushes to the other edge of the dancefloor, where Darcy is bowing off the Colonel and his lady as they launch themselves into the dance, and crowns him with a bowl of caviar which she has picked up en route. All the time she is screeching away in Kraut.

'Caviar,' bawls the Colonel's lady, who takes the rest in her stride. 'That young man is grossly extravagant, Colonel. You must be having a word with him. As for you, my girl,' she says, disengaging herself from her husband, 'we'll have no temperament and tantrum from foreign females of your kind, oh dear me, no.'

Whereupon she knots Lorca into a kind of ball and rolls her through the fire exit.

'Clear that rubbish away,' she shouts in textbook German to the proprietor, and resumes her dance with the Colonel as if nothing has happened.

The party rather fizzled out not long after.

'What went wrong?' I said to Darcy as he and I shared a taxi back to barracks. 'What went wrong with that Heine bit?'

'Just as well it did,' said Darcy. 'Suppose she'd started shagging like a Valkyrie with one and all in front of that old woman?'

'Point taken. A very good job it was that the spell went wrong – but why did it?'

'Well, er. At about eleven I just couldn't resist it,' said Darcy. 'I took her to the loo and spouted Heine myself, which worked a treat. But unfortunately I used exactly the same lines as young Harrison, or he used the same as me; so I suppose she suspected that something was a bit *smelly*, that Harrison and perhaps others had been listening in the loo,

101

... and rolls her through the fire exit

probably with my connivance, or that I'd told them before or after what the form was – at any rate that there was some sort of conspiracy or jape in train. I very much blame myself for not having cancelled our plan ... after my own indiscretion. But I knew you'd start asking questions if I did, and I didn't want to let on that I'd been making the four *fesse* monkey with Lorca – in the lav at that – within three days of my marriage.'

'Don't be so stupid,' I said. 'As if I'd have held it against you. A silly little thing like that.'

'You're right of course, darling. Only I don't suppose my virgin bride would agree. Sweet Lindy – I really must *try* to be faithful from now on. For a month or two at any rate. As to this evening – well, all things considered, no harm done, not this round. That old woman was rather splendid, damping the whole row down in two ticks flat ... but I'm rather afraid, darling, that there's going to be trouble with her. She'll be laying on compulsory Scottish reels five nights a week in the Mess – to spare the poor subalterns the expense of going out and help them save up to get married. Jesus Christ. Bloody marriage. I'm only doing it, darling, because my mother seems to want it so badly ... and what with one thing and another she has been rather a brick.'

En route to the Höhne Ranges
(Spring 1955)

After the premature dispersal of Darcy's party, I managed to be in good time for O.'s five-thirty start the next morning.

'What was going on last night?' he said.

I explained, more or less.

'And you didn't let *me* in on it?'

'What if I didn't? The thing went wrong.'

'That does not obscure the fact that you committed a prior disloyalty by leaving me out of it.'

'For Christ's sake, O. If you want a real worry, start thinking about the Colonel's wife. Darcy says she's going to stick her great snout into everything, particularly into the Mess.'

'Well, for the next three days she won't be able to stick it anywhere near us. You travel up in the back of the three tonner with the boys, old bean. I'll go in the cab with the driver.'

'But surely there's a car for *us*? You always wangle one.'

'I did. The new CO found out and scrubbed it. Up in the back, old bean. There's a good boy, now.'

As we lumbered over the Westphalian Plain in the draughty three tonner, and the cross country runners shrunk lower into their greatcoats, trying to sleep, I reviewed the problem of the new CO.

A lean soldier, this. His predecessor had been comfortable and pear-shaped. But pear-shaped colonels were beginning to go out of fashion. When King Log's reign was over, he had been succeeded by King Stork ... to say nothing of his queen, Boadicea, who had turned up last night. And then again, our time in Germany was nearly done. Rumour said Kenya next. Well, if Kenya it were to be, Queen Boadicea would have to stay at home (under existing regulations) for at any rate the first six months of our tour. Good, as far as that went. But King Stork would be very energetic indeed. Although the Mau Mau rebellion was now over and all that was to be done was to collect the pathetic remnants of the rebels out of the forest, King Stork would see the whole thing as still being on a wartime footing (trust him) and God only knew what disciplinary quirks he might think up, what deliberate and superfluous hardships he might contrive, what sumptuary privations he might ordain ... I was walking through livid jungle with snakes hanging and hissing from poisonous trees and carnivorous orchids snapping at my ankles. A filthy, slimy pond – surely I must have contracted bilharzia through every pore in my body. Crocodiles were gliding towards me with the speed and precision of torpedoes, but now I was out and up the bank just in time (Christ, the stench) and here at last was the Mess and the Mess Serjeant neatly draped in white tropical dress. 'A sextuple

whisky, Serjeant, for the love of God.' 'Sorry, sir: no spirits to be sold in the Mess until further notice. Not even for the love of God. CO's orders.' 'Beer, then; beer.' 'No beer before 1930 hours, sir.'

I awoke sweating with hatred of the CO and his monumental memsahib. We had stopped for something.

'All out for a pee that wants it, sir,' a cross country runner said.

So we stood in a row peeing. The country boys went back

a bit on their hunkers and deployed their parts for all to see, especially while waving away the lost drops. Those from artisan or low, white-collar families in the suburbs of Wolverhampton or Leominster hunched and huddled forward, and held their pricks backhand with fingers spread, as if terrified lest they should fall off if anybody, even their owner, saw them.

Back in the three tonner I asked PTI Colour-Serjeant Plumb, a man whom I knew and liked from cricket the previous summer, what was the reason for this.

'Well, sir,' he began, 'when I was a platoon serjeant in the Recruit Training Company back in Shrewsbury, I had to supervise the showers sometimes, see? And it went like this. Your major public schoolboys from Eton, Shrewsbury, Rugby and the rest didn't mind who saw what. You minor public schoolboys – Bruton, Canford, St. Edward's Oxford, Bromsgrove – they were more fussy (liable to turn their backs while taking off their knickers) – or rather, they were more fussy *until* they saw how the Etonians and the Salopians went on, which they saw was the smart, upper-class way, so then they do let their doings flop about where they would. The grammar schoolboys, sir, what had never left home till now, were very shy but stripped off in the end – though we had trouble with one or two of them that got excited, never having seen anyone else's wanger in all their time, and got bloody great hards-on.'

'What did you do about that?'

'Sent 'em off to cool down. My word for a wank. When we go a little lower, into the secondary school lot, we have a hell of a job getting the knickers off of some of them. Lots of 'em want to wear them right into the shower and even while they're under it. Same with the real rubbish from the towns – much worse. Red with anger they goes if you tell 'em to strip properly. So, sir, if they're going to be bloody-

106

minded, we lets 'em go into the showers with their pants on – and then sit about in wet pants for the rest of the day. That brings most of 'em to their senses, but not all by a long chalk. Some of 'em went on wearing pants in the showers right through to the end of recruit training, and a few still do even now they're here with the battalion. Roughly speaking, it's *those* that cap their cocks while they're pissing.'

'There are some of my boxers here. *They* didn't cap their cocks, as you put it, indeed they frisked them about a bit – and yet they're secondary schoolboys if ever there were.'

'Ah, sir. These here, some of them, are from the rural drafts from Somerset and Cornwall. They're different. There they sleeps whole families in a bed . . . and uses what they've got on whoever's next to them. So they've no call to be shy. During the war, sir, the young mothers down there in the ranges and the fenlands, when their men went away for soldiers, they used to bring up their boys to do the job for 'em, starting from thirteen, so that they'd all know what was expected of 'em when their elder brothers were called up.'

'But that,' I said, 'is rather a special case. What about your working-class townees from Shrewsbury or Wol-verhampton? The ones that won't show themselves or go naked into the showers?'

'*Those* are brought up to consider their dicks as something dirty, sir. When they gets married, they won't let their wives play with 'em, nor will they play with their wives' twotties, because they're thought to be dirty too. It's dirt to dirt, and no touching in between. So dirty are their parts, they think, that they won't even wash 'em in case of contamination to their hands. The upshot is, sir, they think their dicks so disgusting that they won't even look at them themselves, let alone let anyone else.'

'But they must see, from the behaviour of the public schoolboys, (a) that dicks aren't disgusting, and (b) that their betters don't mind showing theirs – so why should they?'

'Well, sir, there's some as gets excited at the novelty, as I said just now. But most still won't touch or look or show, and it gives your low-class boy a chance to be righteous at the expense of the upper-class lot. You know how whores and criminals love to think themselves superior to child-corrupters? In the same way, yer Brummy boy, who can't speak a word that you or I would understand, this Brummy boy thinks he's superior to Master Hoity-Toot from Eton, because Master Hoity-Toot shows all he's got, and yer Brummy or yer Scouser keeps theirs to themselves.'

'There was a boxing match with the Welsh a couple of months back. Their boxing officer ordered both sides to strip right off for weighing in. No one at all objected.'

'I heard about that, sir. Well, your boys were mostly these country boys we've been talking of. As for the Welsh, they were much older men – regulars. Any shyness would have rubbed off them by now, and I don't suppose they've got a lot of righteousness left either. Besides, sir, in a Welsh regiment you know better than to be awkward when the boxing officer gives an order.'

'I can't think why he did it. He wasn't in the least *interested*, if you see what I mean.'

'That'd be Major Hopkins, sir. The whole brigade knows about him – except, it seems, your good self. His wife hides up in the gallery of the gymnasium. She commands him to make 'em all strip. He gets his reward when he goes home to her.'

A halt for haversack rations; for another pee later in the afternoon; and finally we reach Höhne, with just long enough light left for O. and the steeplechase team to walk the whole course.

'I say, old bean,' said O., 'I've got the most frightful head from the fumes in the driver's cab.'

'And I've been half frozen to death, and I've got a raw, red patch on my bum from sitting on a plank. Also piles, incipient dysentery, and probably mange from resting my head against the canvas.'

'Yes, yes, old bean. What you need is lovely exercise. So you just walk the boys round the course with the Colour-Serjeant. I'll do the booking in and the rest. That's an order, old bean.'

This was long before O.'s craze for 'Parafitness' had come on. The sudden inception of that came later, on the road, so to speak, to Damascus. At the time of which I am talking, O. was still agreeably corrupt – though often, as in this instance, at someone else's grievous expense.

'All right,' I said. 'I'll walk them round. But I won't lend you that book. You know, that book you're begging to look at, the *illustrated* one about the Girl Guides' and Boy Scouts' Jamboree, when somebody pours Spanish Fly into the fruit punch.'

O. took out his spectacles, placed them on his nose, and jabbed it at me two or three times.

'I'll report you to the Adjutant,' he said, 'for having such a book in your possession.'

'And I'll report *you* for stealing ammunition from the battalion pistol club to fire for your own private practice.'

'Shame, old bean. Foul. *Sport* must be above such rancour.'

'Gentlemen both,' said Colour-Serjeant Plumb, hearing our voices rise, 'it has been a very long day for you after Captain Halberd's pre-wedding party last night (of which I should appreciate an account later). Why don't you both go and have a nice rest, while I take charge of the team's walk round the course?'

'How sensible, Colour,' said O. 'We'll see to your acco-modation and the rest of the team's, and make sure meals and so forth are punctually available.'

'How very kind, sir. I always say that it is a pleasure to come on these outings with a proper gentleman.'

'Is he often so pompous and smarmy?' I asked, as the Colour-Serjeant and the team moved off down a track and turned into what looked like a bog. 'He wasn't at cricket last summer. Nor in the truck just now.'

'He's laying it on with a trowel,' said O., 'because he and I are in deep complicity. His formality, his sycophancy are a form of irony ... a typical Plumb joke. He is very fond of those, as you will find when you know him better. Meanwhile, you had better know for a start that he has no intention at all of walking those men more than half a mile of that course.'

'But oh I say, O. The honour of the 99th, and all that.'

'Precisely, dear bean. That course is so horrendous that if they once saw it the entire team would go sick tomorrow. And where would the honour of the 99th be then? The only hope is to show them a tiny and quite easy bit, then just shove them in to sink or swim, do or die, when the thing actually starts. Colour Plumb and I have been into all this very closely. Oh, yes, indeedy.'

'But surely ... they won't put up much of a show when they *do* start – if it's as horrible as you say.'

'But at least they *will* start. And before they do I've got some stimulating pills to give them.'

'Really, O. *Doping?* What would Darcy say?'

'He gave them to me himself. They are *health* pills, dear bean, chock full of ... rather unusual vitamins, you understand. Vitamins that make chaps keener, which is of course what vitamins are meant to do. The only thing is ... that these vitamins are arranged in some special way so as to be more effective.'

'Tell that to the judges.'

110

'Old bean, these pills are strictly legit. Darcy had them from some female cousin, with whom he once had a walk out and who's a research assistant in Alchemicals Ltd. No one even knows about them, so they can't be proscribed or illegal. But Darcy's afraid that some busybody may get to know about them pretty soon, and then, he says, everyone will turn all prim about their use by athletes; so this is quite possibly, old bean, our first and last chance to make a killing with them. There are some betting men here from the Guards and the Lancers, and I'm hoping to get 33 to 1 against our lot winning. Colour-Serjeant Plumb will make no secret about walking only a fraction of the course. He'll make a *production* of marching our boys home after the second open ditch – and this should increase the price.'

'We must give Darcy a cut.'

'He's given me a pony to place for him. But of course,' said O., 'since we're bearing all the heat of the day, so to speak, while Darcy is comfortably in a nice safe church getting married, I think we can take quite a stiff commission on his winnings.'

'What about the Colour-Serjeant?'

'He'll find his own market in the Serjeants' Mess. Don't ever lose any sleep about him.'

111

The steeplechase course on Höhne Ranges
(Spring 1955)

The next morning, O. and the Colour-Serjeant collected an official issue of hot cocoa, provided for consumption by competitors after the race. Our team drank theirs before the race, along with a special distribution of 'Vitamin Pills' dished out by O., who saw to it personally that each man swallowed down two tablets with his cocoa.

'Now sit quietly,' he told them, 'until the race begins at 11 am. I know you haven't been over much of the course, but you'll find it quite clearly marked.'

' "Now let it work",' he said to me as we stood near the starting line, on which a whole squadron of official and unofficial assistants were busking and bickering. 'At 11 am our boys will be rearing to go. This effect will be contained, up to a point, until about 11.50, at which time the – er – propellent will shift them into extra-top gear for the last couple of miles. What's the time?'

'10.51.' Our team was already stirring restlessly, eagerness on every face. 'Something is about to go wrong, O.'

'Boyson of the 9th Lancers laid me 700 to a score against our winning, and Wincarnis of the Tins 1000 to 50. *What* is about to go wrong?'

A staff car had just drawn up. All around it the official and unofficial organisers were buzzing and kibitzing. A young Captain of the Coldstream had emerged in boots, breeches and spurs, and was crisply instructing the crowd around him, whereupon they threw up their hands in adoration as if he had been Christ and they his disciples. The staff car departed. The chief busybody then spoke to a RSM who spoke to a CSM who spoke to a staff Serjeant who spoke to

112

two Lance Corporals. The two Lance Corporals began to go round the officers-in-charge of the assembled teams. Eventually one reached us.

'Start delayed till 1145 hours, sir,' he said to O. 'General's orders.'

'But that's an outrage. How can they expect these men to hang around another forty-five minutes in this appalling wind?'

To wind was now added rain.

'No good telling me, sir,' mumbled the Lance Corporal. 'Colonel Saxby-Sonyers' – he indicated the King of the busybodies, the one who had thrown his hands up highest and most fervently in acclamation of the magnificent Guardee – 'Colonel Saxby-Sonyers, he's the gaffer.'

So O. and I went to Colonel Saxby-Sonyers.

'This,' said O., 'is clean contrary to the regulations of the Amateur Athletics Association. You cannot delay the start of an event without giving very good reason.'

'The General has been delayed. As an old hand at cross country running himself, he is particularly keen to see the race from the beginning. He actually did us the honour of sending his ADC to request us to postpone the start.'

'You should have refused. The General's convenience is immaterial. You know – you should know – the regulations as well as I do.'

Colonel Saxby-Sonyers had a face like a parrot and a voice to go with it.

'Who are you?' he squawked.

'Captain O. Paradore of the 99th Light Foot. I *demand* that the race be started at the correct time. I shall muster my team on the start line at 1100 hours, and if no one else comes forward to compete, I shall claim victory by default of the opposition.'

Luckily for Saxby-Sonyers he had an able Lieutenant who

113

had been going rapidly through the compendious book of regulations.

'The thing is quite clear,' said the able Lieutenant (of the Rifle Brigade). 'All Army athletic meetings, etc., etc., are indeed run under the regulations of the AAA; *but* the conduct of such meetings is also subject to all the established processes of military discipline. So if the General says we don't start till 1145 hours,' he said to O. with a look of game, set and match, 'we don't start till 1145 hours.'

'This is disastrous, old bean,' said O. as we returned to our team. 'Those pills are geared to take effect in two minutes from now. Nothing can stop them. By 11.45 they will start to produce final and maximum overdrive. All of which means that most of the energy distilled by them will just have been wasted in waiting about – except for a final spurt of manic ferocity which won't see our lot further than the first two miles or so.'

'Go to Boyson and Wincarnis and suggest that all bets are void because of the delayed start.'

'Why should all bets be void? As that Green Jacket said, this delay is covered by special military regulation. A bloody nuisance and damned unfair but all officially above board. And Boyson and Wincarnis are the least of our worries. I can afford to lose seventy odd quid, twenty-five of which are Darcy's, incidentally, and a fiver yours, but I can't afford to have all our chaps crack up – and believe me, when those pills are burnt out they will crack up – after two miles of the race, having done those two miles at colossal speed. Someone will smell a little mouse somewhere.'

'You say that no one knows about these pills yet. Therefore there will be no test to detect this – er – stimulant.'

'No. But it will look damned odd all the same. Ten men going neck and neck at full stretch, way ahead of the field, for two miles, then all falling flat simultaneously and having to be carried off on stretchers.'

'As bad as *that*?'

'I'm not sure. Darcy's cousin Hetta was very strict with him. "This stuff is harmless," she said according to Darcy –'

'– Well then? –'

'– "*Providing* you make sure that anyone that takes it wraps up very warmly and relaxes totally the moment they stop being active. Even if you can't ensure this," she said, "there will be no serious damage done, but there will be violent and most uncomfortable temporary spasms." You see what I mean? We don't want ten men of the 99th having violent spasms (however temporary) in full public view on the course and all at the same time. As Lady Bracknell said, "It might expose us to comment on the platform."'

'Quite.' I looked at my watch. 1102 hours. Our team was warming up, racing on the spot with vigorous knee-raising, impatience in all twenty innocent eyes.

'A word, gentlemen?' said Colour-Serjeant Plumb from behind us.

'If you please, Colour.'

'Only hope, sir: orders from the battalion to return *immediately* because of some emergency. In such a case, your sporting friends and my own will, I trust, agree to a cancellation of wagers. And the wellbeing of the team will be no problem, if we allow for a little exuberance in the back of the three tonner until all "vitamins" are spent, at which time any tiresome reactions can be easily dealt with by Mr. Raven and myself.'

'Jolly good, Colour. But how and where do we raise an order to return?'

'If you'll pardon me, sir, I always carry a sheaf of such orders, all in the correct format and varied to take account of circumstance, for use at convenience. *This*' – he produced a flimsy wafer of official paper – 'will do the trick. Please return it to me as soon as you have shown it to Colonel Saxby-Sonyers. Such items are difficult and expensive to obtain.'

'We shall have some tricky explaining to do when we get back to battalion,' I said to the Colour-Serjeant while O. went off to Saxby-Sonyers. 'We're not expected back till late tomorrow.'

'Not too difficult, sir. We can spend a night on the way, put the team up in a *Gasthaus*. Then reach battalion at the expected time tomorrow. When asked how the race went, we shall have to fudge up some excuse for withdrawing. Diarrhoea might be best. A sudden onset of savage diarrhoea, presumably caused by something they ate in the cookhouse here last night. The MO this end won't help us, but I think we can persuade Captain Crokers back at battalion to lend support to our story. He still owes the Serjeants' Mess £15 for drinks ordered but not paid for on our last Mess night. To say nothing of other indiscretions, while on his rounds in the married quarters . . .'

'What shall we tell the men?'

'I'll handle them, sir.'

O. came back.

'Saxby-Sonyers looked a bit puzzled but he accepted the authenticity of the order,' he said, handing this back to Colour-Serjeant Plumb. 'So *en voiture toute suite*, I think, before our chaps get any more frisky. Now, these bets. Mr. R.'s and mine are on credit, so we'll discuss *that* when we next see Boyson and Wincarnis. What about yours, Colour?'

'Cash, sir, I'm sorry to say. But in all our interests I shan't try to collect them back just now. *En voiture* is best, sir, as you say.'

So *en voiture* it was. The men muttered volubly in surprise and disappointment, but Colour-Serjeant Plumb's soothing and authoritative, 'You'll hear all about it before long', quelled them for the time.

116

Soon after we left the Ranges by the main gate, our vehicle halted. Colour-Serjeant Plumb, craning his neck round the back, announced that a despatch rider had appeared from somewhere and was talking to Captain Paradore up at the front.

'You see. Just as well we left when we did,' said the Colour loudly for all the men to hear. 'Saved that poor bloody rider a trip through the rain on the Range.'

And indeed the rain was by now torrential.

'You mean, the Captain was expecting a message, Colour?' one of the men asked.

'Of course,' improvised the dexterous Plumb. 'Why else should we have moved out so suddenly? You saw the Captain talking to that Colonel who was running the show. The Colonel told him a message was on the way – that ADC in the riding kit had warned him.'

'What message, Colour?'

'We'll all be told when the Captain has had a chance to get his breath.'

So that was the men dealt with for the next few minutes. They seemed quite calm now. The appalling rain had scotched their appetite for the race, and all this drama about messages and despatch riders and Colonels and aides-de-camp had somehow satisfied their yen for physical action and excitement. The workings of curiosity can be guaranteed to use up large quantities of excess energy.

After a while, the despatch rider came past the back of the three tonner and headed for the guard room by the main gate, presumably seeking shelter and sustenance. The three tonner started down the main road towards the first town on our route back to the Harz, then took an unaccountable turn to the right. Colour-Serjeant Plumb took a long, careful look at the countryside, and then frowned.

'Guess where we're going,' he said to me. 'I've been here before. Belsen.'

'Belsen?'

I looked out with him.

'No signpost,' I said, 'no notice.'

'There wouldn't be, would there? The local authority has had them taken down. They want this site – and others similar – obliterated. As a good-will gesture on our part at the beginning of the new alliance.'

'And what good-will gestures are *they* going to make?'

'They've promised to pay enormous sums, over the next twenty years, toward the rehabilitation of the Jews. Israel and all that. But they don't want this sort of reminder right under their noses.'

The Concentration Camp at Belsen
(Spring 1955)

'This sort of reminder' consisted of four or five long, low mounds of grass, each labelled as the mass grave of anything up to ten thousand unknown Jews, and also of a long low marble monument at one end, on the entablature of which was engraved something, presumably suitable, in Hebrew characters. Under the dense vertical rain the whole thing was immensely unattractive. The three tonner was parked so that we all had a full view out of the tail. The men looked and looked away, not wanting to know.

'Why on earth have we come here?' I asked.

O. appeared to answer. He came round the vehicle draped in a great flapping macintosh cape and climbed up into the back.

'Horrible news,' he said. 'Suitable place to absorb it.'

'Bad news already? But we've only been out of the place ten minutes.'

'That despatch rider at the gate. Read this.'

He handed over a flimsy wafer of paper.

'RETURN IMMEDIATELY RACE CONCLUDED,' I read aloud. 'Well, so we are returning,' I said to O. 'It all fits in very neat. This rain will have flooded the course by now, so the fact that our departure was premature can easily be fudged or obscured.'

'Now unfold the bottom.'

'CAPTAIN DARCY HALBERD KILLED IN ACCIDENT ON WAY TO WEDDING. 99TH OF FOOT SENDING BEARER PARTY FROM STEEPLECHASE TEAM. MUST BE EQUIPPED AND DESPATCHED EARLY TOMORROW REPEAT TOMORROW.'

'That's what comes of faking messages,' said O. 'You get a real one. No aspersion on you, Colour. Your scheme was brilliant. But God had another.'

O. went back through the rain to the driver's cab. The engine started. Mounds and monuments became one with the water.

'Captain Paradore had a very odd look on his face,' the Colour-Serjeant said at last.

'He was very attached to Captain Halberd. They were at Sandhurst together.'

'Not so much a look of grief, nor even of shock. The look of a man who knows, beyond a doubt, that he is called to atonement.'

'Why should he blame himself? That would be totally irrational.'

'So was Saul's behaviour, sir, at Damascus.'

The Harz Mountains
(Spring 1955)

Whatever visions O. had seen or whatever absurd guilt had smitten him, the 'odd look' in his eye was gone by the time we had arrived back at battalion in the Harz. Five days later, after he had returned from accompanying the CO to England, where they represented us all at Darcy's funeral, he seemed fully restored to proper form.

'The Colonel's Mem wanted to come too,' said O. 'She was still banging on about it when I called at his quarters to pick him up for the aeroplane. He told her she didn't know Darcy, and she said nor did he, and he said he was Darcy's CO and had been for a month and more, and she said she'd eaten Darcy's salt – presumably meaning that party – and he said so had a lot of other people but that didn't mean they could all go buggering off to the funeral. The truth is, chums, that she was Darcy's last victim. Clearly infatuated from the first second she saw him.'

'How did the row end,' someone asked, 'between Donald Duck and Harriet Horsecollar?'

We were quick with injurious sobriquets in the old 99th.

'*He* said that the Army wouldn't pay her passage and neither would he. Then she'd pay herself, she said. The flight was booked out, he told her, he'd only been able to get himself and me and the bearer party on the plane by waving black crape around and getting a party of military educational psychotherapists thrown off it. Anyway, she'd only just got here, it was her duty to stay and put his house in order, and that was that.'

'All this in front of you?'

'No. In the sitting room while I waited in the hall. The wall must have been made of cardboard and the door didn't fit, so one didn't miss much.'

'When the chips are really down, then,' Dick Cock said, 'he can match her?'

'I'm not so sure,' said O. 'He won the first hand all right. But at the funeral was the biggest bloody wreath you ever saw, with *her* name on it and *not* the Colonel's as well, thirty-five quids' worth if it had cost a button, and I imagine *he* pays the account at Gorringes' or wherever she'd ordered it from. *And* for the telephone call. And now,' said O., ' "Farewell, sour annoy." For Darcy, he is dead, and that's positively that, so I've arranged a little entertainment to console us all.'

'Us' were myself, Dick Cock, pretty Hughie Long, and Fizzer Harrison.

'We're going to tell all the chaps,' said O., 'particularly Randy Richard, that there is, in Perpendik Strasse, round behind the station, a luscious house of bawds, left over from the dark days when the Krauts sold their sons and daughters for a packet of fags apiece. Not, of course, that it's still as cheap as that now, we'll explain, as they have to pay a bundle to the Military Police for protection, but it's the same good old *esprit* as it was back in '45 and '46, anything goes, all ages and sexes, multiple jobs a speciality. 12A Perpendik Strasse, we'll tell them. Guaranteed by one of the German civilian staff. English cheques accepted if you're short of D-marks. So go one, go all, we'll tell them, to 12A Perpendik Strasse, ring the bell, and say the password – "A soldier is better accommodated than with a wife" (Shakespeare, dear beans, one of those cruds Pistol or Bardolph) when the maid opens the door.'

'And what's in it for us?' said Hughie.

'We,' said O., 'are hiding behind the bus shelter watching them try to get in. And if they do get in, coming out again, which they should do pretty quick.'

' "Matter for a May morning," ' I said. 'One of those

Shakespearean Comedy japes. In real life, O., they always go wrong.'

Despite my warning, the good news is now put about the Mess, and later that evening O., Dick, Hughie, Fizzer and I are hiding behind the bus shelter.

First arrival is Randy Richard. Ring, ring; no answer. Knock, knock. The door is opened; we can't see by whom. Richard utters what is presumably the password as given by O. and passes inside.

'Now watch him being kicked out again,' gloats O.

But he isn't.

Then Orvil Hurstmonceaux and Garry Strap arrive. Ring, ring. No answer. Knock, knock. The door opens. 'A soldier is better accommodated than with a wife,' yells Gary Strap, who is drunk. Drunk and all, they both pass swiftly in. And do not emerge.

'It must be a *real* place,' says Dick Cock. 'How very erection-making.'

'Oh dear yes,' says pink Hughie the Puritan in a strained, unhappy voice, as if confessing masturbation to Mummy.

'What say, beans?' says O. 'Shall we all go and see what's happening?'

'No,' says cautious Hughie. 'Stop trying to feel me up, Fizzer. We must send one of us for a recce.'

'Here am I,' says Dick, 'send me.'

'You're too horny. You'd forget to come back. Hughie is too naif. Raven is just too inept to be trusted with anything. *I* shall go on your behalf,' says O.

'Our hero,' we all cry.

O. crosses the road as bold as Tannhäuser going Under the Hill. Ring, ring; no answer. Knock, knock. The door is opened, once more by someone unseen. A friendly hand (female, we think) is extended and whisks O. inside.

Five minutes, ten, fifteen.

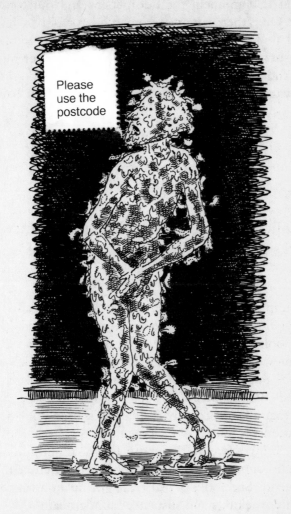

But at that moment the door opens and out totters O.

'The rat,' says Dick. 'He's soaking his member and recks not of his faithful friends.'

But at that moment the door opens and out totters O. Naked. Or rather, covered from head to foot in feathers, secured to his person by some glutinous and semi-transparent substance. No taxi will take him, however much he shouts and bawls about being a British Officer. Poor O. He has to walk all the way up the long, steep hill to the barracks. Alone.

The Officers' Mess of the 99th Light Infantry barracks in the Harz foothills (Spring 1955)

'Very simple,' says Garry Strap later. 'When you and O. put up the trailer for this new cat-house, we sent Orvil down to have a look at this 12A Perpendik Strasse. O. hadn't done his homework properly. There was a "For Sale" notice outside – put there since O. last saw the place, I dare say. Deserted. Bell broken. Cobwebs all over the place. So. We realise that we're being had, that O.'s been rousing false expectations of bliss, and we get the key from the house agent, leaving a five Mark deposit for the night, remove the "For Sale" sign, and park Jimmie (Julietta) Lettice there to act as maid. She looks a real treat got up in a tiny apron, with only stockings and suspenders underneath it.'

'We never saw her,' sighs Dick. 'The door got in the way.'

'Just as well,' says Jimmie (Julietta) Lettice. 'If you'd seen me, you'd have been in there like a pea out of a tube, and then you'd have got what O. got. Treacled and feathered.'

'We thought of *tarring* and feathering,' lisps fluting Orvil, 'but that wath a bit too complicated. Anyway, the idea wath that you'd thee uth arrive and *not* come out, that you'd probably thee Julietta's thighth ath well, that you'd draw the obviouth concluthion and come romping over for nyth nurthery gamieth. We meant to treacle you all, though we knew O. wath the one behind it. In the end, though, we dethided on jutht O. becauthe we knew that you were thuch a rotten lot that tho long ath *you* were all right you'd make him walk up the hill alone, and that would increathe hith punithment. Ith he all right?'

'Just about,' says I, remembering uneasily that the 'odd look' had been back in his eyes when he'd entered the Mess in his feathers.

'Well,' says Fizzer Harrison, 'no hard feelings. It's only such a pity that Julietta's act should have been wasted. Do you think ... an encore ...?'

'But of course, sweetie,' Jimmie/Julietta growls in his husky voice. 'Come to my room in figures ten.'

'Figures ten' meant ten minutes, an idiom derived from radio transmission procedure, which required all numerals to be prefaced by the word 'figures'.

'How many of us can come?' says Fizzer. 'Figures one, two, three ...?'

'Figures *all*, poppet,' growls Jimmie, and lopes off.

'Well,' says Randy Richard, 'they say it's "Hey lads for Kenya" any time now. The warning order came through today. So you'll be kissing goodbye to us National Service lot. We've not got long enough left to be hauled out there.'

'Kissing goodbye is right, it seems,' says Dick.

'Oh yes,' says Fizzer. 'We must say farewell to happy days in the Harz in real style:

' "I'll give you kisses, one, two and three,

125

As sweet as any blossom that blooms along the tree,
As sweet as any ensign in the whole Light Infantry
 For a farewell to Harzburg
 And my days in Germany." '
He looks at his watch.

'Figures five minutes,' he said. 'And then we can knock on Julietta's door.'

Nairobi (Autumn, 1955)

A sight even more ravishing than Jimmie/Julietta in his apron, suspenders and black silk stockings was on show five months later in the bungalow of the Queen of the Uganda Harlots in the centre of the out-of-bounds (i.e. red light) area of Nairobi.

I had got there with a gambling acquaintance from the Muthaiga Club who was the General Manager for Tusker Beer in Nairobi. Since the harlots consumed large quantities of Tusker, and my friend made a point of being companiable with substantial clients, it followed that he was quids in with the head Uganda whore, who owned several houses to which his firm made frequent deliveries. Thus he was a person of great consideration in the red light district and could absolutely rely on being given girls that were not diseased (about 80% were) or even virgins for the asking. He had caused a sixteen-year-old maiden to be placed at my disposal for 60 Kenyan Shillingi (£3) and hence the engaging spec-

126

tacle to which I have just referred: nice plump calves (the connections of harlotry were well nourished while they lived), long silky thighs, pert little paps, a right tight but juicy slit below a small, strong *mons veneris*.

There were, however, two factors to impair my felicity. In the first place, were I to be caught out of bounds by the Military Police, I should be court-martialled and probably cashiered. True, I was in civilian clothes and carrying a civilian passport (the one which I had obtained as an undergraduate and had cunningly preserved with the entry of my occupation unaltered); true, furthermore, that the Tusker Beer man would tell any nasty interloper that I was his employee: the fact remained that once seen I should not be forgotten and was almost certain to be recognised on some subsequent occasion.

My second worry was that my principles debarred me from deflowering young girls, even if they were (or were said to be) over the age of consent, if only because I dislike causing pain and creating mess. While this aversion need not spoil my pleasure (for there were plenty of appetising amusements that did not entail penetration) it might expose me to the disdain of the girl, or of her colleagues, or, most invidious of all, of the Queen herself, who might then take it out on my Tusker acquaintance. Here have I been to the trouble, I could imagine her saying, of providing this most pure piccaninny, and all your screeny friend can do about it is to lick her buttocks and come between her tits. What the hell are you, Raven, I could imagine his then haranging me: some kind of fairy? Though he must already know the answer to that one, I thought, as he had asked the Queen to offer me boys as well. These I had refused, but only after careful inspection and then by reason, not of their gender, but of their faces, which were like those of treacherous pie-dogs. The virgin, on the other hand, had a jolly and pleasing

127

little countenance; and so far from being affronted when I did not couple with her, was quite delighted, remarking that she would still be able to charge the price commanded by the intact from her next customer. (It seemed that the Queen, an amiable and humane woman, did not suffer her girls to be 'sewn up' and passed off: once you lost your cherry in this quarter, that was that, and your price immediately dropped by about 40%, like that of a new car the moment it has been paid for.)

All in all then, my second and social anxiety was a non-starter. But the first was still palpitating away, increased many times by *tristitia post coitum* (or, more precisely, *tristitia post ejaculationem*). I sat on the front bench of the Tusker merchant's Triumph while he finished his own business with the Queen, head right down, praying that no Land-Rover would draw up and emit red-capped figures ('Well now, sir, a civilian passport we have here; and perhaps we have a Military Officers' identity card as well, or was it *someone else* that hit two of my balls running for six, in our match against the 99th Light Infantry?'). Things were not improved when my little virgin opened the car door and snuggled in with a younger sister (or so she was introduced), apparently ready and eager for a replay, 'so that 'er can see what 'appens with youse wangy'. The idea was so inflammatory that very soon I had a double dose (so to speak) of *tristitia post ejaculationem*, and had to put my foot down when one of the girls opened the door of the car and whistled up two of their little brothers, suggesting that another exhibition of manliness would be in order. However, my foot did not go down very firmly (it had been many weeks without rain and the proposal was one of enticing perversity) and soon three pairs of dark eyes were gleefully watching their elder sister at work on my anatomy while three pairs of little dark hands got to work on their own. In the middle of this madness, the

128

Tusker merchant appeared, cleared the decks with a short and very sharp imperative, and drove me away towards licit territory.

'You mustn't muck about with the kids,' he said.

'I didn't. They just kind of appeared out of the floor.'

'I know. There's not a lot one can do to stop 'em, the way they swarm. Like that scene in the children's brothel in some poem by Verlaine. Or was it Rimbaud? Of course the Queen and her people don't give a damn, but if the Kenya police ever found out there'd be horrible trouble. Colonials get very sanctimonious about this sort of thing.'

'Doesn't everybody?'

'I don't. I'm just warning you, that's all. Nairobi races next Saturday?'

'Alas, no. I'm only down from the Forest to sit on a court martial. It'll be all over tomorrow, and I'll have to go back.'

'No chance of spinning it out? What's the chap up for?'

'Caught out of bounds. In the red light district,' I said. 'All cut and dried, I'm afraid. Even if I were the President, I couldn't spin it out beyond tomorrow.'

'What'll he get?'

'Two months' detention. Perhaps three.'

'Why don't they give your boys brothels of their own, vetted by the MO, so that they can have it off cushy without going out of bounds? That's the least you can do for them.'

'I agree. So have a great many other officers over the last one hundred and fifty years. But the Great British Public does not. The women in particular are afraid that their husbands and sweethearts might get horny and pop along for a bang. The Bishops are no help either. Such brothels have quite often been organised – but some sneaking prude with a grudge about something always blows the whistle, and *then* watch the heads tumble into baskets.'

'What are the chaps supposed to do then?'

129

'Go out with Mrs Palm and her five beautiful daughters. And play ping pong in the intervals.'

'Do they go for each other?'

'Sometimes. But not much. The British provincial lower classes are rather chary of that. And once again, if they do have it off with their mates, there's always some worm in the grass to report them. Generally someone who's in trouble for something quite different. It makes quite an effective red herring, you see. If a man goes to his Company Commander and puts on the virtue, saying "I saw Corporal Box with Private Cox's prick in his mouth, I abominate such behaviour and find it my duty, sir, in the circumstances, to come to you" – if a man gets going in that line, you've got to *pretend* to be grateful and regard him as a defender of British morals; and it is expected that you should reward him in some way, generally by forgetting one or more of his own serious misdemeanours.'

'What do *you* do when that happens?'

'I did have something of the kind occur while I was still commanding a platoon. The delator expected me to take it higher. Luckily I was able to propose a deal. The informer had been caught thieving a day or two before. "You forget what you saw in the Lance-Corporal Storeman's bunk," I said, "and I'll forget the two quid you stole from Private Horrocks." What he wanted, of course, was to have the theft forgotten *and* to star at the trial of the Lance-Corporal Storeman; but in the end he accepted my terms. Nasty bit of goods, Midlands Low-Church puritan through and through. Threatened to report *me* at one stage for trying to hush up immorality.'

'How did you get out of that?'

' "Listen," I said. "These men are my friends and should be yours. You can't really want them put in prison just for a bit of slap and tickle." Oh, but he did all right. Ranted about homosexual vice and corruption and God knows what. So then I had to take another tack. It so happened I knew he was a bit finicky about dirty work – coal fatigues and so on. "Look," I said again "I am asked to recommend a man for permanent employment in the cookhouse. Unblocking drains, garbage disposal, that kind of a thing. Unless you drop all this, it'll be you. Now, you just forget all about the Lance-Corporal Storeman, and I'll forget all about Private Horrocks's two quid (when I've paid him back myself) and you'll stay here and keep your hands clean."

' "No cookhouse, sir?"

' "No cookhouse."

'So he agreed to the contract. I waited a month – by which time it was too late for him to report the Lance-Corporal Storeman, because he'd have been asked why he'd delayed so long – and *then* had him sent to a permanent job in the showers and latrines. I wanted the swine out of my platoon, and technically I'd kept my word. "No cookhouse," I'd promised him. And no cookhouse it was – but the shit house instead.'

'Well, well, well,' said the Tusker busker as we drew up at the guard room of the 99th's camp in the suburbs, 'such goings on. And all because the Army Council listens to a load of spiteful women in England and won't allow battalion brothels.'

'I've cobbled together something in that line for my own Company in the hills,' I told him. 'Enthusiastic local girls. Trouble is, my medical orderly is no Doctor Wasserman, and some disaffected bastard may open his bloody mouth at any minute. Meanwhile, I've got the lowest VD rate in the division.'

'Heigh ho,' commented the Virgil of the Nairobi Inferno. 'Let me know when you're down again – if they don't throw you in the slammer for running a disorderly house. Next

131

racing after this Saturday is in four weeks. And we might have another evening out.'

'Right you be,' I said, half yearning for it and half dreading it.

But in the end there were no more evenings out. The Tusker fellow had his head chopped off with a *panga*, by one of the last effective Mau Mau soldiers, a certain 'General' Kumo, who had taken shelter in the Queen's domain (unknown to her) and rushed out in a fit of fanaticism to execute the white man who had just been 'insulting African womanhood'.

Christ, you poor sod, I thought, when I read about it in a week-old newspaper up in the Aberdares: that *panga* would never have gone through in one go, the 'General' must have been hacking away like a woodcutter. There but for the grace of God, I thought, go I; and went no more to the Court of the Queen of the Uganda Harlots.

Lake Naivasha (October 1955)

But even in Kenya there were other amusements. O., now promoted Major, was running a kind of Intelligence Centre on the edge of the Aberdare Forest. He had Company Serjeant-Major Plumb (as he now was) and a staff of two drivers and two soldier-servants. These had been perfectly trained to run a *parti* of roulette – one as 'Chef' in a high chair, two by the wheel at the head of the table, and one

132

down at the bottom. A gaggle of old chums, including Dick
Cock and Randy Richard (who at the last moment had taken
a regular commission and come with us to Kenya) went out
to spend the night at O.'s new pleasure dome.

We were received by CSM Plumb. He had always looked
rather gnomelike in the face – tall, upright and limber but
nevertheless gnomelike in feature – and now he looked
more so than ever. Pinched, for all his height and well
proportioned body. Trouble was clearly in the air.

'Now, gentlemen,' he said, 'Major Paradore apologises
that he cannot be here to receive you. He has been called
out to deal with a case of indiscipline in one of his pseudo-
gangs.'

'Pseudo-gangs?' we said.

'A method invented by Captain Kitson of the Green
Jackets, sir, which Major Paradore is developing and
improving. A group of loyal Kikuyu – loyal to us, that is –
feign fellowship with the Mau Mau, get to know their
intentions, and reveal them to this office. Thus we are able
to track down and capture rebels much faster – which is to
our advantage *and* theirs, as they then no longer have to
wander without food or weapons in the Forest. You realise,
gentlemen, that for a long time now the only commodity
that has been plentiful with the Mau Mau is the pox –
distributed in abundance by the whores their agents kidnap
from the towns to serve them.'

'Well, what's gone wrong with this pseudo-gang?' from
Richard.

'One member has defected to the Mau Mau. Most unusual.
These days it is usually the other way about.'

'When will Major Paradore be back?'

'Impossible to say, sir. But dinner will be ready at eight-
thirty, and there will be roulette at ten. He has left funds
with me to pay winners of up to £25. Those winning more

133

will have to claim from him.'

'So you don't really expect him back?'

'He may be back, sir. He has made provision in case he should not be. That is all I can say. Our usual complement of croupiers will be reduced by one, as one of the drivers has of course gone with him. But as there are relatively few of you, the game should proceed quite smoothly.'

The substance of all this was well enough. Of course O. could have been called out suddenly by the exigencies of his job; of course apparently loyal Kikuyu could defect; of course roulette could proceed smoothly enough with three croupiers instead of four. It was Plumb's manner that bothered me. The man was not his usual easy self. He was stiff and correct – not by way of irony, as was sometimes his wont, but because he had a beastly wicket to bat on. He clearly wished that we had not come. He also knew that we had every right to come, having arranged this affair with O. some time before and not having been warned off. He was therefore determined to use us right. There would be dinner and roulette; winners would be paid up to £25 in cash and could have the rest on subsequent application to O. Plumb could be more affable. But then he was evidently nervous and upset. What was going on?

As the evening went on, matters improved a bit. Dinner – tomatoes *provençales* and local game with very passable wine from South Africa – was a credit to the establishment. Roulette, though we had little heart for play in O.'s absence, was deftly conducted by the two soldier-servants who had provided dinner and by the reserve driver who had acted as wine waiter. They knew their job as croupiers and enjoyed it, the more so as O. would pay them a percentage of his profit (if any) and as we observed the Continental custom of tipping them in the event of a win *en plein*. The CSM watched us and occasionally (although house manager, as it were) applauded a lucky win; but as with us, his heart wasn't in it. All in all the thing went off quite well but it was heavy going.

Then, just before midnight, O. came in. We rose to greet our host. He looked at us with sorrow and disappointment, natural enough in the circumstances, and we waited for his account of what he had been doing. It did not come. He waved us down into our seats, watched the next two or three *coups* with an expert eye to make sure the croupiers were doing their duty properly, then once more put on his look of disappointment. But now it was quite clearly disappointment, not at having missed the greater part of our visit, but at the spectacle of our behaviour, as though he would have reproved us if we had not been his guests, as though he repudiated the very entertainment while he himself was providing for us.

'Good night,' he said in an artificial voice, as though he were reading a text before a sermon. 'Enjoy yourselves. Breakfast tomorrow will be at 0900 hours.'

Then away to his private quarters: not a word more. After a short while the CSM followed him and did not return. By common consent play was abandoned. The croupiers began to pack up the roulette kit.

'We was to give it all to you, sir,' one of them said to me. 'The wheel, the cloth and the counters. We shan't be needing them again, the Major said.'

'But surely . . . he's not leaving here?'

'Not as I know, sir. But he says we shan't be needing this again. Pity. We've enjoyed the Major's roulette parties.'

'Do you think . . . we can see Major Paradore before going to bed? I'd like to thank him for this very handsome present.'

'Leave it till the morning, sir, if you please. These days, when he says "good night" he means it.'

'These days?'

'There was a time he didn't mind being knocked up again,

135

sir, if someone came late, one of the Kenya Rifles as might be, wanting a drink. Not now. Leave it till the morning, sir. Please.'

The man was pleading. So we went to the rooms which we had already been allotted, found hot water bottles in the beds, very welcome in the heavy damp of the Forest, and small decanters of whisky set on the bed tables with the storm lanterns. A high standard of hospitality; a very low standard of greeting and friendliness; what could it all mean?

At breakfast the next morning (eggs and bacon, Dundee marmalade, tea, chocolate or coffee) we were told that Major Paradore had long since left on the day's rounds, taking the CSM with him. We had to be back in Nairobi, thence to be driven to our respective Company camps on the other side of the Forest, at one o'clock. And so, just after ten, we packed our grips and O.'s roulette equipment into our vehicle and, having first tipped O.'s servants, sadly and thoughtfully departed.

'Do you remember,' said Dick Cock, as we rumbled down the escarpment and turned left for Nairobi, 'the colour presentation two years ago? Soon after we arrived in the Harz?'

'Vividly,' I said. 'I had to take care of the photographers and the pressmen. Never before or since have I heard so much poisonous whining in the space of twenty-hour hours.'

'Did you see much of O. about then?'

'Not a lot. He was too busy getting his drill together for the great day.'

'At that time,' said Dick, 'he was second-in-command of "B" Company. My Company. So I saw a good deal of him. He wasn't just getting his drill together, as you put it. He was working himself into a dreadful emotional state about being worthy – worthy of the occasion, of the colour, of the Sovereign who was, if only by proxy, presenting it. One had to be worthy in body, he once told me, which meant being totally fit and alert and absolutely *pure*, and also worthy in mind, which meant more purity (one must not admit even the *notion* of carnal delights), total reverence of the Sovereign, and a willingness to die *instanter* if She commanded it. The whole thing was weird. He behaved as though he thought he were Sir Galahad. And it's not as if he was carrying one of the colours or playing an important part. All he had to do was to trail round behind the Colonel of the regiment, standing in for the ADC which he, as a retired General, had not got. He didn't even have to draw his sword, yet he spent hours practising sword drill. And all the time he had on his face the same look as he had last night – reproachful. Reproachful of us who were not being worthy but were even making jokes about it all. He did not reprove us, nor did he make any effort to co-opt us into his sword drill and so on; he just looked ... disappointed in us. The nearest he came to actual rebuke was when that little wretch, Garry Strap, told us one morning at breakfast about how a German tart had given him a blowjob in a telephone kiosk the night before. While Garry was going on about this with some elaboration, O. got up, took the photograph of the Queen off its hook and put it back with her face to the wall. It quite put Garry off his stroke.'

'So what does all that prove.'

'That O. has ... well ... puritanical interludes, during which the usual amusements, comments and pleasantries are taboo.'

Randy Richard capped this tale with one about how O. had suddenly developed an overriding enthusiasm in his training of a company Rugby XV.

'No fun, no jokes, no alcohol, no sex, not even an evening out at the Garrison Cinema. Relentless it was,' said Randy Richard. 'And then, after we'd won our match, the whole craze was just forgotten. There was another match due

'O. got up, took the photograph of the Queen off its hook'

soon – a more important one, in the Brigade Company League – but O. just lost all interest. He handed over the rugger to me, resumed a normal O. sort of life, and didn't even turn out to see our next match.'

'It was a bit like that after the colour parade,' said Dick Cock, 'except that he not only forgot all the chivalry and purity charade but absolutely made jokes about how seriously *other people* had taken the whole thing. "Dear little Hughie Long," he used to say. "When he was carting the new colour up the line he looked as if he'd discovered the Holy Grail." Reduced poor Hughie to tears.'

I too recalled an uncomfortable incident. We were on leave together in Venice, when suddenly O. remembered that it was his mother's birthday in four days' time. As a rule he had few good words for his mother, who was a mean old woman subject to ridiculous health fads, but the approach of her birthday now induced a fit of matriolatry which endured right up to the night of the birthday itself. Cards and presents were sent off registered and expressed at appalling expense, candles were lit in churches, and there was even some question of commissioning a special Mass.

'For Christ's sake,' I complained, 'you're not a Catholic. Neither is she. In fact you told me once she was half Jewish. Shall we set something up in the synagogue in the Ghetto?'

This tasteless joke was received with the look of reproach or disappointment we had all been commenting on, but otherwise no remark was made. In this horrible air of *agape* we continued until the day of the birthday was actually done. At dinner O. had proposed 'a little private toast to the most marvellous mother a man ever had'; as soon as the clock struck twelve he said,

'That old bitch of a mother of mine is trying to do me out of an eighteenth-century carriage chronometer which my father left to me, to me by name, in his will. It's worth at least a thousand quid. *She* says my father changed his mind on his deathbed and told her she was to have it. I say that since this never got into his will, and she has no witness of what he said, the thing is incontestably mine. So does the lawyer. She's gone and hidden it somewhere. I'll have to get a court order to make her produce it. I rather hope she refuses, as it would give me enormous pleasure to have the old cow slammed into gaol.'

'All right,' said Dick Cock when I had finished this anecdote, 'so what's got into him *now*? I mean, what has set this mood off here in the Aberdares? It can't be rugger or colour parades, not in the jungle. Do you suppose it's his mother again?'

'No,' I said. 'We're safely past her birthday.'

'Well . . . just his mother in general?'

'It could be anything,' I said, 'from the Mau Mau (perhaps he's sorry for them, or thinks they should be honoured in defeat) to some new vision of himself as Cecil Rhodes.'

'Connected with Kenya then? Or at any rate with Africa?'

'Not necessarily. It could be some delayed infatuation with the Captain of the troopship we came out on ("What a fine service the Merchant Navy is," he said to me in Aden), or a book he bought in Port Said about Egyptian ideas of immortality, or a photo he's found at the bottom of his old kitbag of a dog he had in his nursery. It could,' I said, 'be absolutely anything at all. The chap who'll tell us what will be CSM Plumb – when we can next get him on his own.'

Nairobi Races (November 1955)

Some three weeks later was Nairobi Races. Luckily I had another court martial to attend (this time I was defending a man who had thrown his edition of Marx at some humbugging chaplain), one which would continue after the weekend. Since it stopped at noon on Saturday, I was in the paddock in good time for the first race. And there too was CSM Plumb, stepping trimly through flowerbeds towards me.

'Down from the Forest?' I said.

'That's right, sir.'

'And Major Paradore?'

'Keeping the show going up there,' said Plumb lightly but dully. 'Told me to take the weekend off.'

'How is he?'

'He has a new passion, sir, for Christian names. Up there, we all have to call each other by our Christian names. Not for friendliness – the men and I would hate that, however friendly we may feel, if you follow me – but for security.'

'In which case you and the men don't feel too bad about it?'

'I suppose not, sir. The idea is that if we all take off our badges of rank and call each other by our Christian names, the enemy won't know which of us is which. As to that . . . well, perhaps . . . and perhaps not. The trouble is, sir, that I am very sensitive about my Christian name.'

I remembered his initials from some order: 'L.R.' Surely, 'L' could not stand for anything too disastrous. If it had been 'X', 'Y', or 'Z', or even 'Q', there might have been cause for disquiet. But 'L' was surely harmless.

'I'll tell you about it, sir, if I may, so that you'll understand how I feel.' For a moment Plumb's face was more gnomelike than ever. 'Initials "L.R.", sir, as you may know, standing for . . . standing for "Lazarus Risen".'

'Oh . . . Couldn't you use something simpler, less portentous? Peter would retain a biblical ring, if that was thought desirable, while Richard or Henry or George would convey a nice sense of the continuity of English history.'

'You're making fun of me, sir,' said Plumb without resentment. 'I can't say that I blame you.'

'I'm sorry, Sergeant-Major. I was simply nonplussed. But quite seriously, couldn't you change your Christian name – at any rate for use up in the Aberdares?'

'A Christian name, sir, is given. If one repudiates it, one repudiates the givers, that is to say one's parents. My parents were as decent and kind a couple as ever lived in Ledbury. True, they were perhaps overstrict as Wesleyans, and got carried away by their enthusiasm in the matter of my Christian baptism; but I do not see any reason, on that account, to snub them by rejecting the name they gave me.'

'Very well spoken. A most honourable attitude. But meanwhile, your – er – present nomenclature is rather a mouthful. What do you think Mau Mau infiltrators will make of it? Will they think it's some kind of ju-ju?'

'Though I cannot disown it,' said Lazarus Risen, 'custom allows me to abbreviate it. So Major Paradore and the rest of them have shortened it to "Laz", and "Laz" in careless diction has become "Les" ... and no one can say there's anything ... portentous, as you put it, sir ... about that.'

'No, indeed. A very sensible solution.'

'Except, sir, that I hate the name like poison. It belonged to a young cousin of mine – female – who used to pinch my bottom in chapel.'

'Lucky old you.'

'She did it to mortify, sir, not to stimulate. That grey mare has just had the most enormous crap. Always back a horse that craps in the paddock.'

'Absolutely, L–Sorry, I mean Serjeant-Major.'

The grey mare – Naughty Nineties – won by a head at a 100 to 7. (In those days that was what we said instead of 14 to 1: much more stylish.) We had won over 700 Shillingi (£35) between the pair of us and agreed to bet in syndicate for the rest of the afternoon. We then put a tenner on Auntie

Mabel, which for all I know is still running over the Ngong hills, and in the third race a tenner on Aesculapius, which, inappropriately, burst a blood vessel. Funds were now getting low; but a fiver on Georgy-Porgy at 4 to 1 put us ahead again, and it was decided to risk £15 in the fifth on the even money favourite, Lars Porsena, a black stallion with regal bearing.

As we walked from the paddock under the palm trees to the stand, CSM Plumb said:

'Remind me to tell you a few things about the Major, sir.'

'I thought we'd be coming to that.'

'After the racing's done. No point in spoiling that.'

'So the news is ... bad?'

'Dreary, sir, as Captain Halberd used to say. "Dim, dismal and dreary, Colour," he used to say to me: "Roll on death." A joke idiom, sir, as we know: but it seems Someone was listening.'

'Well ... We'll hang about after the last race and go into the Major then.'

Lars Porsena lay last round the bend under the ilex and into the straight, but as soon as it was asked paced past the rest of the field as swift and sure as an angel cruising.

'Fifty quid in the kitty,' said Lazarus Risen. 'Shit or bust, sir?'

'Shit or bust, Serjeant-Major.'

'Now then, sir. I saw King's College Chorister win quite easy over a mile last time I was here. You were at King's College, weren't you? Before you came to us.'

'I was.'

'Then it looks like a direct hint from God.'

'I'm not sure. I did not leave the college in circumstances of esteem. No scandal, you understand, but one or two mild misunderstandings about money. Also, the place is beginning to become "dim, dismal and dreary". Secondary socialism, you know the kind of thing.'

'I can imagine it, sir.'

'If we want a pointer from God,' I said, 'what about Horace Horsecollar? Number five.'

'Never won a race, sir. Unplaced every time he's been out. Best result eighth of eleven in a real dogs' race last autumn. Anyway, where's the pointer from God?'

'The Colonel's lady,' I explained, 'was nicknamed Harriet Horsecollar in the Mess, because her name is Harriet and she resembles the Disney creation, Horace.'

'Yes,' said the CSM, 'I remember. As a child I had one of those books which you open at the middle and all the characters stand up. *Mickey's Annual* it was called. Mickey Mouse, Minnie Mouse with huge, high-heeled shoes, Donald and Donna Duck, Goofy and Pluto, and dozens more that are never heard of now. Clara Cluck, Clarabelle the Cow, and sure as God made cider apples, Horace Horsecollar – with an enormous halter.'

'That's it. When the CO's wife wears her pearls they look like Horace's halter. Hence the name. And hence the pointer, There's much magic potency in a name.'

'Colonel's wife hasn't come out here yet, sir. Perhaps her potency may not be enough, all the way from England.'

'*Her* potency would be enough all the way from Saturn.'

'Right, sir. Fifty quid up on Horace Horsecollar. Ram Chowdah over there has 25 to 1 on his board. Shall we take it?'

Ram Chowdah went a bit white at the prospect of losing £1,250, but it is, after all, a very distant prospect.

The mile start at Nairobi is on the far side of the course (at any rate as it used to be). The horses run clockwise with the rails on their right: straight for four furlongs, then round a fairly sharp bend which is overshadowed from the left (as they run) by some tall and graceful ilex, then, for the last

144

three and a half furlongs, between groves of box, palm and casuarina, and up to the finishing post in front of the Aberdare Stand (with its traceried colonial verandahs), though these days, no doubt, it is called the Kenyatta Stand, or something even more unsuitable and irritating.

Every dog has its day, and this day would appear to be Horace Horsecollar's. Lying third up to the bend, he nips ahead as the bend begins and leads by four lengths out of it. Down the straight towards the winning post. But here comes King's College Chorister – a huge, powerful brute, ridden by a black jockey with bare feet; he accelerates away from the rest of the field and begins to catch Horace.

'Hold on, Horace Horsecollar,' yells Plumb; 'if you win you can fuck my sister.'

'The jockey, I suppose you mean.'

'Of course, sir. The horse is a gelding. And at least the jockey's white ... unlike that bloody little nigger who's catching him.'

Up comes the bloody little nigger on King's College Chorister, who sneaks upsides Horace on his left flank, and just gets his face past on the post.

'*Cunthooks*,' said Lazarus Risen.

'Never mind,' I try to comfort him, 'all we've lost is *their* money.'

'Think what we might have won, sir.'

'Oh yes ... if I want to go mad. Let's go round to that bar behind the bandstand, and you can tell me about Major Paradore.'

Our own Regimental Band was signing off with The Post Horn Gallop as we passed behind the stand. The Bandmaster grinned at us through the oscillations of his baton.

'Back that one?' he called.

'No,' said Plumb.

'King's College Chorister,' the Bandmaster called after us,

145

'just had to do it with me in the music game. Had a fiver at 4 to 1.'

'So he wins twenty,' said Plumb, 'and we are within a foot of twelve hundred. It couldn't have been a dead heat, sir?'

'First,' crackled the loudspeaker system through the Post Horn Gallop, 'number one, King's College Chorister; second, number five, Horace Horsecollar: third, number four, Sail to Cyprus.' More crackling, rather frantic. 'Objection,' honkered the loudspeaker, 'objection: the second objects to the winner for bumping and crowding.'

'Ballocks,' said Plumb. 'That little nigger took King's College Chorister a good four foot wide of our nag. He won it fair and square, that little nigger did.'

'That's not the point,' I said. 'The point is, here in Nairobi, that he *is* "that little nigger". Tell about Major Paradore.'

'In deep gloom, sir. His favourite expression just now is a line from Shakespeare's Sonnets, "The expense of spirit in a waste of shame". That night you all came for roulette, he kept out of the way deliberately: simply didn't want to see and talk to his old chums. And you know what he did when he went to his room? What he always does – hundreds of press-ups and much swinging of bloody dumb-bells. Stands on his head for ten minutes at a time. I have to go in and stop him before he has a fit.'

'What set all this off?'

'Hard to know, sir. But there *was* some business back in the Harz, I gather, when all of you had some kind of jolly together – and the Major was left out. He's very obscure about it all, but he comes out, from time to time, with something about having to cleanse himself in a bath while you all enjoyed yourselves without him. He's none too clear what you all did, but he bitterly resents having missed out on it. He had an idea you deliberately kept him out, chose a time when you knew he'd have to be in the bathroom.'

146

'Ridiculous,' I said. 'It all just – er – fell out that way.'

'Of course it did, sir, and so I tell him. But it still rankles. So now he's off, sir. He's leaving us. He's applied for a posting to some parachute mob.'

'He's never done any jumps.'

'He's taken to practising off the roof at our centre. "Must be Paraready, CSM," he says. "Paraready and Parafit." That's his new phrase. "I'm off to do some real soldiering," he tells me. "Purity and parafitness, that's the ticket," he says, "and none of this sloth and wine-bibbing and wallowing in the mire." Sometimes he reminds me of my father when under full sail, sir: "Woe to the unrighteous and to the whore-masters, woe to the followers of Baal."'

'Objection sustained,' bawled the loudspeaker, 'objection sustained. King's College Chorister is disqualified and placed last. New placings: first, number five, Horace Horsecollar; second, number four, Sail to Cyprus; third, number ten, Three Coins in the Fountain.'

'Jesus,' said Plumb. 'They might at least have let that poor little nigger boy keep second place. Even if he interfered with our horse – and he didn't – he certainly didn't go near anything else.'

'You forget,' I said. 'Just as the jockey on Horace Horsecollar was white, so was the jockey on Sail to Cyprus.'

'I really don't wonder, sir, that these nogs want their own country for themselves.'

'Neither do I.'

'Well, sir. In all the circumstances I shall be giving a bit of my winnings to some good cause. What do you think of Kenyan independence?'

'Tactless, from one in your profession and present cir-cumstances. Can you think of nothing else?'

'My parents' chapel runs a charity for fallen scout masters.'

'A very kind thought.'

'How much should I give, sir?'

'A tithe is generally considered appropriate.'

'A tithe, sir? Only a tenth? After all, we've won our money by a sheer fiddle.'

'It wasn't our fiddle.'

'Nevertheless, we have profited by it, sir. We have touched pitch. The only way not to be defiled by it is to give *all* our winnings away.'

'To fallen scout masters? Talk about touching things, they've got a bit to answer for.'

'Very well, sir,' said CSM Plumb, signalling to the barman for a third quintuple scotch for both of us, 'you have convinced me. I shall keep half. I may even invest it on the market when we get home. To England: land of fair play and fallen scout masters.'

Saturday before Easter 1987, Tweasledown Races (near Camberley)

'And did you?' I said to Major (Quartermaster) L. R. Plumb (Retired) a generation later.

'Did I what, sir? Sorry, I mean, Simon.'

'Invest half your winnings in the market? *Or give* half to fallen scout masters come to that?'

We were at a military point-to-point on the course at Tweasledown. The only reason I was there was that JBB was doing the commentary on the races, so James and I had come along to lend him company and encouragement. Just for once God (i.e. the gods, Fate, Chance, or Fortuna) had a pleasing dividend in store for me, in the shape of Colonel O. 'Parafit' Paradore and his old mucker, Serjeant-Major, now long since Major, Plumb. O. I had not seen since the backgammon fiesta in Deal some months before: he looked less whoozy than he had then but still a bit groggy. Plumb, who had driven him down from London, I had not met since Horace Horsecollar day in Nairobi.

'Long march no see, sir,' Plumb had said when he first saw me in the Tweasledown paddock.

'"Simon" now ... don't you think?'

'Yes ... Simon. Lucky this. I met old O. at the regimental dinner last night. Hadn't seen *him* in a long while, either. We agreed that I should drive him down here. I gather his little misfortune in January will prevent him from driving for some considerable time to come.'

'Possibly just as well. Fill me in on what's been happening to you.'

'Well ... to begin at the beginning, I did not invest any of my winnings at Nairobi in the market, or give any of it (God help me) to fallen scout masters. I went back and gambled with it on the course. And lost the lot. I could have cried.'

'I know the feeling,' I said.

'But the real reason, Simon, was not my racing losses. Only money, as you say. My sadness was that by that time O. was gone and so were you. You can say what you like about O., and certainly he has his peculiarities, but on a good day he's tremendous fun to be with, and anyhow I'd known him since he first came to the battalion with Darcy. Next to Darcy I loved him most. Anyhow, by the next time I went down from Naivasha to Nairobi Races, O. was back

149

in Aldershot getting more and more 'parafit', and you was back in the depot, supposedly training the recruits but in fact, as we all heard later, bankrupting yourself on every racecourse from Aintree down to Chepstow, and I was still stuck in Kenya, about to become CSM of Headquarters Company, the dullest job in the world.'

'What happened to your Intelligence Centre?'

'They scrubbed it out, soon after O. left ... without even appointing a new officer i/c. I arranged the funeral, so to speak. There was no need, you see, of any more pseudo-gangs or amusing tricks like that; no more need of intelligence. The whole Mau Mau thing was over. All we had to do was bring 'em in and clean 'em up and settle 'em down somehow till the blacks took charge – and to be fair the blacks in Kenya did it pretty well, when you compare their form to the fuck-ups everywhere else in Africa. We'd been instructing Kenyatta on the side, of course, while he was in prison, and he had the sense to listen.'

'Madame Kenyatta wasn't much help to anybody.'

'All she suffered from was greed. At least she didn't want to reform people or make them equal or anything as silly as that.'

'And when you left Kenya?'

'Usual sort of thing. Postings to the Territorials in Hereford and Ludlow. Posting back to regimental HQ. Postings to the battalion, in the Middle East, then in Germany again, then in Scotland, Germany yet again (horrible by now, with all the Krauts getting above themselves), the whole scene getting smaller and smaller, fewer and fewer places to go to, Northern Ireland suddenly brought into the act but who the hell wanted to go there? And all the time, Simon, everyone getting more and more pofaced and pedantic and goody-goody and "efficient", more and more "technologically minded", less and less capable of making or enjoying a joke, shit scared of doing anything that might affect their miserable, dreary careers, forever passing the pisspot to someone else and hoping that he'd spill it, so that his enemies could kick him in the face while he was trying to mop up. And all so deadly serious, so earnest, so *pi*. Christ, how I longed for a breath of Darcy or O., that lot, your lot, *the old gang*. But you'd had trouble with the bookies and Darcy was dead and O. was off parachuting and Dick Cock resigned to take the family business over when his elder brother died and Randy Richard got multiple sclerosis. For a time I used to see little Hughie Long, who was a Territorial with the battalion in Hereford, and we'd have a glass or two and a crack about the old days, but then he got married and went away to live in Cumberland. Oh, he asked me to his wedding, and to me it was a wake.'

'You seem to have had a pretty dismal time, er ... er ... Do you still abbreviate yourself to "Les"?'

'No. I started using Lazarus in full about twenty years ago, because that's what I began to feel like. Better dead than risen, I used to feel some mornings when I got up; but then I'd remember that old saying, you know, "This day too will pass as all days pass in the Army", and I'd say that out loud three or four times while I was shaving, and it's quite astonishing how much better it made me. So day after day I did my work and minded my business, kept my nose clean, had an occasional modest flutter ... was eventually promoted to RQMS, then to RSM, and was finally recommended to old Donald Duck, now Colonel of the regiment, for a Quartermaster's commission.'

'So it turned out all right in the end?'

'For what the thing was worth, yes. But oh the boredom. And the nagging. After 1960 the whole thing changed completely. Don't do this, you might kill someone; don't say that, you might offend someone; don't drink at lunchtime;

151

get married, we don't approve of bachelors; get children or all the other NCOs will be jealous that you're not buggered up with kids like they are; get a smaller car, that one will cause envy; wear a hat at the races, it's the done thing; don't wear a hat at the races, we don't do the done thing any more, it isn't progressive and modern. You couldn't even have a fart in the rears without someone clocking it in a log book.'

'But you didn't get married ... Lazarus?'

'No. It nearly cost me my commission. That's to say, when my name came up for one they wanted to know why I was still single. Lots of sly looks. You know.'

'What did you tell 'em?'

'That I'd had a fiancée who was killed in a nasty motor smash, and never cared much about anybody afterwards.'

'As good a tale as any.'

'True ... in a way. Anyhow, they shut up about all that. After I was commissioned life was even duller than before. Imagine it ... fucking ledgers all day long ... in the Quartermaster's stores. Stink of feet and stale cigarettes. No open air. The odd game of cricket ... till I went and laughed at some twit that was wearing a crash helmet to bat in. I ask you: a crash helmet in an inter-battalion cricket match. The CO had me in afterwards and said I wasn't being sensitive to the modern point of view. Young men wore helmets to play cricket in, he droned, because it helped them to "identify" with their heroes in the first-class game. This made for personal fulfilment. Such "aspirations" must be respected. Pure make-believe, and that was the sort of wallop you had to listen to all day long. I tell you, Simon, those slow horses of yours did you the best turn ever: they saved you twenty-five years of utter and total tedium. Like some version of hell, worked out by one of those sadistic old bastards who wore hairshirts and never washed. But ... "This day too will pass as all days pass in the Army." That's the only thing that kept me going.'

James came up.

'Colonel Henry for the first race,' he said to me.

I introduced him to Plumb. Then, 'This is Major Lazarus Plumb,' I told him.

'How do you do, sir,' shaking hands. 'Colonel Henry, I think, for the first race.'

'Thank God for decent manners,' said Plumb, as James departed to put a tenner for each of us on Colonel Henry, 'when you can find them.'

We went to fetch O. from the bar and tell him about Colonel Henry, waited while he backed the horse and walked out to the third last fence from home, which was in a dip. The centre of the course was heath and pine, with hillocks and copses that blocked one's view wherever one stood; so one did better to concentrate on one fence and get full value from that.

James joined us, having got odds of 4 to 1 against Plumb's tenner and mine. O., who had got only 3 to 1, started to sulk. A heavy silence descended.

'At least,' said James politely and apropos of nothing, in order to get conversation going again, 'as far as one can make out, *pimps* don't come to point-to-point meetings. Sandown, in one's experience, would have been full of them, giving their whores an afternoon out.'

'Tell you what, though,' said O., restored to good humour by this topic, 'the place is full of nasty little yuppies with their nasty little wives.'

'Yuppies?' said Lazarus Risen.

'Mucky young beasts on the make. Pulling in money so they try to put on a bit of class. One of them over there has a circular revolving wine rack with twenty different kinds of wine on it. On my way to the bar just now I asked him

153

'I asked him if it played a tune'

if it played a tune as it went round. He looked as if he was going to hit me.'

'They take themselves very seriously,' said James. 'They want you to think they're really Sloanes.'

'Sloanes?' said Lazarus Risen.

'Real class; or rather, something a bit nearer to it.'

'Who are those two having it off then? Yuppies or Sloanes?'

'Just yobs,' said James. 'A yob and his *bit*. Sometimes called *piece*. They come to point-to-points near London in order to steal. Most proper people, at this sort of meeting, leave the boots of their cars open. Yobs help themselves.... when they're not having it off with their bits.'

'Or pieces,' said Lazarus Plumb.

154

'I hope they steal that revolving wine rack,' said O. 'But why can't they get into their car to do their rutting? Or go into the trees?'

'They hope someone will try to stop them,' said James, 'then they'll make a thing of it. Freedom of expression. Human right to love. Healthy youth and down with hypocrisy. All that.'

JBB's voice came over the heath from the commentator's tower.

'Approaching the fourth fence Colonel Henry is going third and very easily.... Half way round the first circuit ... and so to the open ditch. Momma's Boy, Just Jake, Colonel Henry.'

I thought of my humiliating attempt to ride round this circuit in the pentathlon, thirty-two years before. Did O. remember? I wondered. I looked at his face and decided that he did not.

The runners came past us for the first time.

'That brute on Just Jake is hitting much too hard,' said O. 'He thinks the stewards won't see him down this dip.'

Just Jake fell in front of us.

'Serve you right,' said O. to the rider, 'hitting your horse like that. Pity you didn't break your bloody neck.'

O. had obviously made good use of his time in the bar.

The rider approached, eyes blazing, whip at the ready.

'What's that about my bloody neck?' he said in a vile Kentish urban accent.

'Pity you didn't break it,' said O., 'flogging your poor animal like that.'

The rider stalked closer.

'Four against one, chummy,' said Lazarus. 'On your way. I know one of the stewards, and I'll report you to him for brutal use of the whip ... unless you clear off now.'

'It's quite true,' continued Plumb as the rider receded. He

155

held up his race card, showing the cover. 'O. knows him too.' O. glanced at his race card, clearly puzzled. 'You remember: Lieutenant-General Sir Crambo Breeches Boyson, the chap who laid you seven hundred to a score against our winning the steeplechase at Höhne. Boyson of the Lancers. One of the old gang. When we had to leave in a hurry, he decided we hadn't come under orders and let you off the bet. Unlike that jumped up grocer, Wincarnis of the Tins.'

'Yes,' said O., 'I'm beginning to remember. Wincarnis never got his money, you know. He sent me a letter in which he claimed it, but the very next day he was crushed by a scout car while having a strain in dead ground somewhere. Driver didn't see him till too late.'

'Dead ground it certainly was,' said Lazarus Risen, 'as Dick Cock remarked at the time. Dick had heard a rumour that the driver really did see Wincarnis but deliberately didn't stop; and that a Cornet of Horse, who was in the vehicle, said "Well played, Trooper Bloggs, we can all do without that bugger." Everyone hated Wincarnis, who was as mean with his cash as the Jew of Malta, and so nobody in that scout car ever let on what really happened to him. Some joker that composed the epitaph wrote that "Death overtook him as he was striving to do his duty". You know, I really think,' said Lazarus to James, 'to judge from your old man's commentary, that Colonel Henry has a good chance.'

We waited patiently till the runners came into sight again, about a furlong down the course, and then clumped past us. Colonel Henry, in the lead, was being pressed by a chestnut with a very pretty little girl on top.

'I'd love to ride *her*,' said O. glumly, 'but my riding days are done.' And to Plumb, 'Do you think we ought to seek out Boyson?'

'No,' said Lazarus Risen. 'One of the old gang he may

have been in the old days, and certainly he behaved very sportingly about that bet; but to have become a general officer in the modern Army he must have turned into a mealy-mouthed martinet a long time since.'

'I don't know,' I said. 'The other day I met a marine who's just been promoted Lieutenant-General. Head of the whole marine kybosh. He seemed rather jolly.'

'He'd better not be jolly in the Army's time,' said Plumb, 'nor even out of it if anyone can see him, or they'll scrub his appointment before you can say "Alf's Button".'

'I thought nobody read that book nowadays,' I said.

'They wouldn't if some of the librarians had their way,' said Plumb. 'It's fascist, don't you know? I just managed to save the copy in the Mess library at the depot. The education officer wanted it thrown out because one of the marines makes a heavy joke about niggers being backward.'

We were all well punished for Plumb's racialism (or should one say racism?). Colonel Henry was beaten by a short head. JBB came down from his tower to meet us as we walked in. He had heard from me of O. and Plumb, though he had met neither, and was much intrigued by them. He brought the intelligence that a man called Naylor Leyland, who was determined to top the point-to-point Jockey's League for the season, would be flying in by helicopter to ride a 'certainty' in a later race, a horse called Sheater.

'That sort of rich behaviour,' grumbled O., '*not* what we want at this kind of meeting. Helicopters, indeed. I very much hope that the brute loses.'

He did – and flew straight out again. Good riddance. All of us were then saved by Deep Cross (James's selection) at 5 to 1. A quiet afternoon (apart from O.'s fracas with the flogger) and a pleasant one. An autumnal feeling, although it was spring. Something to do, I suspect, with O. and Plumb ... both of whom have now been invited down by JBB for

157

the Trog cricket matches in Kent this summer.

'Backgammon then,' said O. as we said goodbye.

'You're trailing a bit. Two monkeys down. The invitation to play at my club is still open.'

'This cricket in Kent will be quite soon enough, thank you. Come along, S'arnt-Major Plumb.'

O. had been to the bar again.

'Coming, sir,' called Plumb, with a brief look of youth in his eye.

May 22, 1987, Hunstanton golf course

'You to hole this putt, Chancellor,' said Peter Walter Budden to his partner.

Peter Budden was JBB's younger brother, built like an oil drum of flesh and bone. The Chancellor (a sobriquet) was a highly placed and highly dubious civil servant, who was believed to be involved in somewhat squalid spying under cover of bottomlessly boring research. They were playing as partners in a foursome match against myself and JBB on Old Hunstanton golf course. Four up with four to play, they now needed to put down this nine inch putt on the fifteenth green to halve the hole and clinch the match. Whichever side won would stand the other dinner this evening (our last) in the best restaurant on the coast, which was beyond words deplorable.

The Chancellor squared up to the putt. Said JBB,

'A sassy bit lass of Dundee,
    Slipped into the kirk for a pee.
        When they said, "Use the loo",
        She said, "Knickers to you;
    I likes squirting in front of JC." '

The Chancellor gave something between a snort and a giggle and missed the putt.

'Three down and three to play,' said JBB to me.

'You are not allowed to disturb your opponent,' said Peter Walter Budden (henceforth PWB).

'And you are not allowed to blaspheme on the golf course,' said the Chancellor.

'You did both the other day,' said JBB, 'when you told that story of how Jonty went on your brother's honeymoon and they all had it off in the south transept of the church of Kingsbury Comitis, under the monument to the Seventh Earl of Taunton, who was kneeling in prayer with his very buxom wife and their twelve children, five of whom were carrying their own skulls. They got the key from the rectory, you said, opened up the church, locked it again on the inside, and started feeling each other up in the narthex.'

'I must remember that word,' said PWB. ' "Narthex". Rather a good euphemism for the private parts. My boys are getting fed up with "pudenda" and "aidoia" and "pubes". "Narthex" has a nice new ring to it. "Shut up, Slob Minimus, or I'll kick you in the narthex." They'll enjoy that sort of remark.'

'The narthex,' said the Chancellor, 'is a loggia or portico at the extreme west end of a church, between the west door and the commencement of the nave.'

'Pity,' said PWB, and lit his thirteenth tube of the afternoon as we went on to the sixteenth tee.

To our left the sea, at low tide, lapped the beach on the

159

far side of the sand dunes. To our right an easy slope rose from the tee to the spine of the green, gorsey ridge which divided the course north-east/south-west all the length of its lay-out between Old Hunstanton and Holme. In front of us, and slightly downhill, a hundred and eighty-five yards away, lay the sixteenth green, guarded, flanked and backed by small bunkers like Japanese bowls.

JBB to drive for us: a high mashie shot which the wind caught and carries forward into one of the little bowls of sand behind the green.

'When are you going to give up those hickory-shafted clubs and buy proper modern ones?' says the Chancellor to JBB.

'When I get a decent win with Coral.'

PWB to drive for their side. He has two kinds of stroke: a short, whacky swing with his woods; and an even shorter stabby swing with his irons. He judges this to be an occasion for a stab with his No. 5 – and rightly so. His ball drops like a plummet some four feet short of the hole and stays absolutely still.

'Fine shot,' opines the Chancellor. 'Must get a half, even if Raven puts his bunker shot dead. Dinner on them, I think.'

'For what that's worth,' gripes PWB.

' "The man that once did sell the lion's skin," ' says JBB, ' "Was killed with hunting him." The trouble is, Chancellor, that even if I do get a decent win with Coral, I shall have to pay out most of it for James's dinners.'

'James's dinners?'

'Peterhouse has more dining clubs than the whole of the rest of Cambridge put together. James apparently belongs to all of them.'

'Come, come, man. Only three guineas a go,' pontificates the Chancellor as we walk slowly down the ridge and through the spiked gorse towards the green.

160

'That's 1950 prices,' I emend. 'More like thirty guineas a go these days.'

'At the Beef Steak before the First War,' contributes PWB, 'every undergraduate dining had a double magnum of champagne placed in front of him in case he should get thirsty in the intervals between the service of all the other wines. Going it a bit. I wonder what that cost?'

'A guinea a head for start,' says the Chancellor, 'traditional fee for clearing up the honk.'

My bunker shot skims the rim of the bunker, pings across the green like a racquets shot, hits the pin, falls straight down along it into the hole.

'That for a half,' gloats JBB at the Chancellor, pointing to his tiresome four-foot putt. 'Now then:

> 'A grammar-school boy called Traherne
> Was very determined to learn;
> So he said to the Head,
> "With my sister in bed
> Should I come up her front or her stern?"' '

The Chancellor's putt, dead on target, stopped a quarter of an inch from the hole.

'Two down and two to play,' says JBB to me. 'Heads still above water. Great show. Carry on, Mr. Midshipman Easy, and all that.'

'Three guineas for a club dinner in the 'fifties,' I sigh in reminiscence. 'Grammar-school boys that wish to learn, like your Master Traherne. It all comes together, you know.'

'How?'

'We had two grammar-school boys in King's in my day ... in the early 'fifties, that was.'

'I think you'd have rather more if you were there now,' says the Chancellor. 'Not even grammar-school boys. Comprehensive or secondary. The nastiest and dirtiest they can

161

The Chancellor's putt ... stopped a quarter of an inch from the hole

find in the whole of Great Britain. Where possible, black.'

'Our two were white enough,' I proceed. 'They were called Coggins and Birkenhead. They wanted to belong to absolutely everything going, in order to learn how to behave there.'

And now the fen mist creeps across the lawn and up the River Cam, obscuring the summer golf course and the lazy sea, bringing me back to King's, the easy, civilised, wining and dining King's of the Michaelmas term in 1951, not the socialist snakepit they keep there now.

King's College, Cambridge, S.R.'s tale of the two tyros (November 1951)

'Oh yes,' I told my companions, 'they wanted to learn all right, Coggins and Birkenhead did. So among many other Circles and Societies and Associations and Fraternities, they joined the King's College Ten Club, which read plays aloud once a week and also had a magnificent Christmas blowout, by special subscription, after which we'd read a joke play like *Where the Rainbow Ends* or *Peter Pan*, with much drunken improvisation. Well, in 1951 the cost of a decent dinner, with sherry first, two kinds of wine, a third of a bottle of port per head, beer *ad lib* during the playreading – the cost of all this was, precisely, three guineas a head plus a ten per cent gratuity for the college servants that waited on us. Rather good value, we all thought. So did Coggins and Birkenhead, a genial couple who were quite determined to see how one of these affairs was conducted, being very keen on rising from their own social level to one several floors higher. No rot about sticking with the people from whom you sprung in those days. Coggins and Birkenhead had already developed quite creditable voices, not exactly Eton but no worse than Stowe; they knew about not wearing the collar of your games shirt plastered down on to the collar of your blazer; after twenty-four hours they'd dropped the word "toilet", indeed almost overdid it the other way, talking about the "pisser" and the "crapper"; they didn't called the dons "sir", but "Dean", "Tutor", "Provost" as the case might warrant, and managed just the right sort of intonation, one which implied that even the Provost was little more than a rather privileged upper servant; and now here they were, coming to their first big club dinner.'

May 1987, Hunstanton golf course

And so to the seventeenth tee. Par four; fairway rising towards the crest of the ridge, back the way we'd just come. A passable but rather wide drive from me (to the right); a lucky scuffle for the Chancellor, which hopped along the ground for about a hundred and thirty yards, out of the rough in front of the tee and dead straight towards the hole. The green is just short of the spine of the ridge, which meant that PWB had a shot of about two hundred and fifty yards (with a lot of run in the ground) and JBB one of about two hundred, from a very awkward position (as we now realised) behind a gorse bush.

'In the old days,' I remember, 'the green was down on the other side of the ridge. At the bottom of it. You had to play a very long, blind second.'

'Why did they change it?'

'Bloody professionals. They won't play championship golf on a course unless they can see the bottom of every pin as they play their approach shots.'

'Pampered prima donnas. Go on about this club dinner.'

'Two days before the thing was to happen, E. M. Forster (talking of pampered prima donnas) got himself in on the act. You may remember that he spent the last years of his life at King's as an Honorary Fellow, economising. Nothing to do, of course, except polish up some book about one of his great aunts.'

'What about the queer novel, *Maurice*?'

King's (November 1951)

'*Maurice* had been finished years before. It was a five-star blushmaker, and he must have had the sense to know it, so it stayed rotting at the bottom of his trunk (as it should have done for ever), leaving him nothing to do until death except make a bit of trouble when he saw his way to it. Which he did here. As a member of the Ten Club himself, he wrote to the President and said that three guineas was an "obscene" sum to pay for dinner when nine-tenths of the world were starving. Which confused poor Coggins and Birkenhead very much when they heard about it. Because Morgan Forster was a very big name, they'd learnt all about him at their grammar school, and if *he* thought something was wrong about this dinner, then something probably was wrong. We explained to them that it was just Morgan's way of getting out of paying his own three guineas, since he was so tight he couldn't bear to pay out of his own pocket for so much as a cup of tea; but Coggins and Birkenhead still weren't quite convinced.

' "Look here, Coggers," said the secretary, "the fact is that you've both paid up for the dinner, and you won't be getting your money back if you don't eat it, because I've lost every penny of the subscription on the November. Buck's Fizz, curse every leg of it. The bloody thing somehow hung itself on the starting gate just as it went up."

' "Oh," said Birkenhead. "Then how will you pay for the dinner?"

' "It'll go on my college account, Birkers," said the secretary, "and stay there."

'Coggers and Birkers exchanged significant glances. Another important lesson, vital to class levitation, had been learned.

' "So boys," said the secretary of the Ten Club, "you've both paid: it'll be a bloody nice dinner, I promise you that: a load of laughs, with Dudie the Dean ad-libbing as Peter Pan – he says he's getting up a scene in which he persuades Wendy to suck him off. So stop listening to the old woman that lives in her shoe, and turn up at seven of the clock for seven-thirty next Friday, should God let us live so long." '

May 1987, Hunstanton golf course

PWB took his whacky wood swing and put the ball on the near edge of the green.

'Fine shot,' said the Chancellor. 'Now we've really got them.'

JBB took his cleek

JBB took his cleek, or some such thing. He was that much nearer the hole than his brother had been, and although he had to play right under the ball (in order to clear the gorse bush) he got enough length to land on the green and roll up to the hole – dead.

'Labia,' apostrophised the Chancellor. 'Red, writhing labia. What happened about your dinner? I hope you all pissed in your beds afterward. Or worse.'

King's (November 1951)

'That's as may be,' I tell him. 'We're concerned with *before* the dinner, Chancellor. With the moral struggle, in the minds of Coggins and Birkenhead: should they follow the Master and eschew the dinner because it was an insult to the starving multitudes; or should they bask among the fleshpots and watch, or at least listen, to the enactment of Wendy Darling sucking off Peter Pan, meanwhile themselves picking up much (more or less) upper-class lore about the correct idiom and usage for such occasions?'

'Well: what did they do?'

'They rang up the Headmaster of their grammar school, there no longer being time in which to write and be answered, at very considerable expense. "A point of conscience, Headmaster," they said, carefully not calling him "sir" because that would have been middle class. And then they explained their dilemma. "Don't be so ridiculous," their Headmaster said. "My Staff and I have not sweated and laboured to get you two into King's in order that you should pick up that sort of rubbish from ninnified dilettante socialists. I *command* you both to go to that dinner."

'So they did. And the first person they saw when they got there was E. M. Forster. It turned out that he had been invited as the guest of the club, which apparently made it quite all right vis-à-vis the nine-tenths of the world that were starving. The reason why he had been invited was that one of the committee had remembered that a year or two before he had played a marvellous Wendy opposite Dudie the Dean's Peter, and would clearly be exactly right for the promised new scene of fellatio.'

May 1987, Hunstanton golf course

'Of all colleges in the kingdom,' said the Chancellor when he had failed to put down his thirty-yard putt and had conceded the hole, 'yours is the silliest. Maynard Keynes, marrying an imbecile Russian dancer and bankrupting a third of Europe with his theories –'

'– He didn't bankrupt the college. He made some very shrewd investments in South Africa –'

'– And that ludicrous Kahn, bankrupting another third,

168

and then some Hungarian – Balogh, was it? – finishing the job. Wasn't Keynes queer, by the way?'

One down and one to play. The eighteenth a par four. A wide fairway to receive the drives, but a deep and concealed Smugglers' Way running from the beach and just in front of the green. Both JBB and PWB put immaculate drives up the centre, leaving the Chancellor and myself with easy No. 3 iron shots, to pitch over the Smugglers' Way.

'Some story I recall,' said the Chancellor, 'of Keynes' falling in love with the college chaplain. Or the other way round.'

'There's nothing about that in Roy Harrod's biography.'

'They went on a holiday together,' insisted the Chancellor, 'and persisted in staying in youth hostels. They were both over forty and Keynes was as rich as Midas.'

'I don't think that can be true,' I try to put the record straight. 'But there was someone else, in my time, with a name very similar to Maynard Keynes, who did indeed have an affair with one of the college clergymen. Both dead now. The clergyman used to pretend the other chap was Rupert Brooke.'

My three-iron shot sails over the Smugglers' Way, pitches in the grass just beyond it, and trickles on to the green.

'Fine shot,' says JBB.

The Chancellor puts his ball into the Smugglers' Way.

'Play another?'

'Certainly not. That path is a *thoroughfare*,' orates the Chancellor, 'and not a hazard. In which case we are entitled to pick out without penalty, drop our ball this side of it, and play our *third* shot.'

'I've been playing on this course since I was in knickers,' I tell them. 'We came here every summer before the war and *lived here* after it. The Smugglers' Way has always been treated as a *hazard*.'

'My dear fellow, that's not what the rules of golf say. If there is a recognised *thoroughfare* across the course, and your ball is on it, you can either play it as it lies or pick off and drop without penalty.'

'But here we always say that this is a haz —'

'— It doesn't matter what you say. Local custom cannot void the rules of the game.'

So the Chancellor and PWB picked their ball out of the Smugglers' Way and dropped it. PWB put the ball six feet from the pin. JBB then put our first putt dead: down in four. The Chancellor had his putt to halve the hole, thereby winning the match and dinner.

'No stupid limericks this time,' said the Chancellor to JBB.

'As you say,' said JBB. Then to me, 'Wasn't that potty dancer whom Keynes married called Lydia Lopokhova?'

'Something of the sort.'

'Then how about this?

Keynes
Had so many brains
That it left some over
For Lopokhova.'

The Chancellor smirked and missed the putt.

'Harassment,' said PWB. 'My partner stipulated no rhymes.'

'He stipulated no limericks. I gave him a clerihew.'

'Halved match,' I said. 'Dutch dinner this evening.'

May 1987, the Club House, Hunstanton

'Do you know,' said the Chancellor as we walked up to the terrace above the eighteenth green, 'when my sister put in her Dutch cap one night during her honeymoon, Jonty didn't know what it was. My brother had to explain to him. Even then Jonty got it mixed up, and thought that Dutch caps were the same thing as French letters, and vice versa. So when he was having a walkout some time later with that Field Marshal's daughter, he gave her a French letter out of a packet which he'd bought from a machine and invited her to put it on, as if it had been a Dutch cap. "I wore one yesterday," Jonty said. "Your turn today." The girl thought she was being sent up and made an hysterical scene. She had a prominent clitoris, you see, and thought Jonty was suggesting that the condom should go on that. Pity that girl broke it off: she had seventy thousand from an uncle – good money in those days. Is Jonty playing for the Trogs this year?'

'There's been a bit of trouble,' said JBB. 'I'll explain at our Dutch dinner.'

May 1987, The Three Cutlasses
by Hunstanton

'Jonty Delaware,' said JBB over our sardines on toast (first course), 'spent several years during the late 'sixties and early 'seventies as an assistant master at Lord of the Isle Preparatory School. PWB, as an expert on all such schools, can now give you a rundown on the place.'

'So called because it is on a commodious island in the middle of one of the lakes,' PWB said. 'Boys and girls from seven to thirteen: a few delinquents – sacked from their public schools, etc. – from sixteen to A-Level. A great reputation for getting people through exams of all kinds, as the school is listed as "remote", so that the papers are sent over a short time in advance for the candidates to take them *in situ*, and the Head Opens them up as soon as they arrive and prepares his pupils accordingly. Many satisfied parents on that account, but trouble pops up on others. The delinquents from the senior school molest juniors, matrons, maid-servants and local livestock with impartial and remorseless regularity. Pot is imported. The Senior Master goes on periodical gambling jags in northern casinos, and is not available for days at a time. The Headmaster, Proprietor and Founder is, or rather *was*, one called Peter Seagrams, the brother of a modish journalist, a Catholic not lapsed but continually lapsing, omnisexual in his tastes and much given to whacking for ill measure. He was married (before the place crumbled entirely) to rather a good minor actress, but carried on a permanent liaison with the science mistress, whoever she might be at the time, because he adored doing it in the labs – all those implements and things, one supposes. He also used to bribe the head boy of the junior school with

172

jumbo sized Mars Bars to fabricate accounts, out of a mixture of fact and fantasy, of what went on in the dorms.

'But to those that didn't know what *was* going on in the dorms the place was instantly and wonderfully attractive. When you crossed to the island by boat, you would land on a pretty little quay and proceed along a path between box trees to a Georgian building shaped like an "E" without the horizontal stroke in the middle and thus making a three-sided courtyard, with a small obelisk at its centre. Behind this building, a terraced lawn sloped down by easy stages to ample playing fields which were, still are for all I know, surrounded by oaks and beeches and past which, at the far end, a brisk stream, full of trout, flows through copses of fir and ilex.'

'Hither,' said JBB, 'came Jonty Delaware to play cricket for the Trogs one summer, for at that time, over twenty years ago now, we used to take an XI in August to stay there a week or more, Seagrams being one of our keenest members and delighted to let us use the place as a country house, playing sides from all over Northumbria. Idyllic, thought Jonty ... who was fresh out of Worcester College, Oxford, and in search of a teaching post. However, instinct warned him on no account to teach at Lord of the Isle, for Seagrams' reputation was shady, not to say unsavoury. On the other hand, he *liked* Seagrams, for who could help it? The long curly hair, spreading monk's tonsure, fresh pink face, apt and light quotations from the European classics, absurd, lofty leg breaks, the reminiscences (entirely genuine) of National Service as a Guardee, the friendly jokes, the open hand – oh yes, Seagrams was an attractive fellow all right; and Lord of the Isle, seen in tranquil August with no pimply, pot-smoking pubescents or beaked furies that taught gym and handcrafts or puffy-faced ushers – Lord of the Isle, I say, was an attractive school, dozing in the early autumn

173

sun while the babbling stream went by behind one as one fielded at fine leg. And there was a vacancy for a junior classics master. And the money wasn't bad as money then went. And it was all so easy to arrange, and would save Jonty any further search for employment, and there would even be a modest advance to tide him over the remainder of the summer hols, and travelling expenses would be paid from his home in Somerset, and the end of it was that before the Trogs parted and left the Lake District for that year Jonty was fully signed up to take on his duties at Lord of the Isle on September 19, just under a month away.

'All that,' said JBB, 'was more than twenty years ago, long before Jonty's affair with Field Marshal's daughter and even before he made a third on the Chancellor's brother's honeymoon. And how, you well may ask, does any of that affect the possibility of Jonty's turning out for the Trogs this summer? Time has gone by, it is many years now since the Trogs have played on Seagrams' island, Seagrams himself is long dead – aye, *there's* the rub.

'You see, Jonty *adored* Seagrams – adored him and loathed him. The sight of Seagrams in yellow (genuine flannel) trousers, tossing up his leg breaks or playing a hissing Malvern slash, sent Jonty into frissons of joy. The sound of Seagrams, behind his study door, whipping little boys of nine and ten (on their bare bottoms, Jonty knew, for Seagrams delighted to publish the matter) made Jonty sick with anguish. And then the school was a slag heap; and honest Jonty hated the pot and the cheating and the sight of infants haggard with cold (the last cheque to the coal merchants having bounced as high as the moon), hated the Senior Master, who put his damp hand in the tuckshop cash box and greased off to Carlisle to piffle the sixpences away at Black Jack, hated the lavatories which never flushed and the filthy drudge who never cleaned them – God, how Jonty hated the Lord of the Isle and all that therein was. And yet he stayed. For every year, through the next five years or so, with August came the Trogs and the London Caterers to this island paradise, which was temporarily cleansed of whippings and of ink-stained fingers mutually masturbating and of sluts that taught Hist. and Geog. and radiated BO. Every year Jonty found that he could just endure the long winters and the cruel springs so long as he knew that August would come and with it the good days, the cricket days, the sylvan fly-fishing days, as they had been when he came first to the Lord of the Isles and first met Peter Seagrams.

'And so we come to the mid-'seventies. 1974. That year was the year of the Tontine. The Tontine (incorrectly so named) was a pool into which any Trog that wished paid a tenner, on the understanding that at the end of the tour (i.e. at the end of the sojourn at Lord of the Isle) half of the kitty would be awarded to the Trog who had made most runs and the other half to the Trog who had taken most wickets. Both Jonty and Seagrams fiercely, fanatically, obsessively aspired to win *both* prizes. Since in those days the Trog tour comprised ten days in Kent, eight in Somerset, four in Hereford and Shropshire, and between eight and eleven at the Lord of the Isle (a total of well over a month, surely the longest amateur tour ever) a serious contender for the Tontine had a very long and tough row to hoe. Most Trogs came and went, cut a match here and there, "rested" for a day or two, went racing in Shropshire or riding on Exmoor: but neither Seagrams nor Jonty, such was the scope and fury of their ambition, could afford to miss a single match. Yet some they had to miss: I couldn't let them hog places all the time. And certainly I couldn't let them hog the batting and bowling. Quite apart from casual Trogs who always looked forward to the odd game every year, there was a formidable band of regulars. Raven here and his brother, who was still with us then, PWB and his friends from Oudenarde House in Sandwich, where he taught, also Hare and Rochester and Torrington and Biffy Gibbs from Tonbridge, Cannon and Gropius and Fairhaven and Webb, and indeed myself, who, when all is said, was and am the captain of the Trogs, and still fancied a game in those days. There were, you see, plenty of good men and true to be kept happy, never mind Jonty and Seagrams.

'So eventually I devised a formula to deal with them. They could both play, I said, in four matches out of five. They could both bowl eight overs a match at first change; and they could bat one and two and ten and eleven in alternate matches. A rough and ready scheme but the best I could do. As for the other five contenders for the Tontine, they must take their chances as they found them. There would be plenty of play for them too: but in the case of Jonty and Seagrams, of this pathological, this almost psychotic rivalry, I had to see that they both had guaranteed and equal opportunities. They were playing, you might say, for each others' soul; to him (if either) that won the double event would go not only the title of champion but the rights of moral arbiter: if Jonty won, he only had to speak the word and there would be no more hideous striping of poor little buttocks or murky concubinage with grunting viragos in the labs; but if Seagrams won the Kingdom of Hell would endure forever, and Jonty be bound (by some curious unspoken compact) to teach on at the Lord of the Isle until his death. For no reason that you could name, the thing had gradually inflated itself into quasi-cosmic dimensions: starting as a mere friendly test of skills, it had become a mystic duel of angels.'

A cheeseboard of sweaty nasties was set before us and at once waved away.

'Quadruple cognacs to make up for the horror of dinner,' the Chancellor said.

176

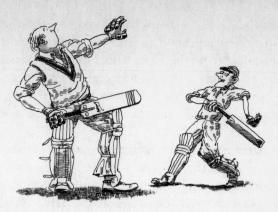

'Amen,' *cantant omnes*.

'So,' said JBB, 'to cut down a long, ferocious and often boring story, when Jonty and Seagrams came to the last match of the tour at the Lord of the Isle, Jonty had an aggregate of 882 runs, Seagrams of 901; while Jonty had taken 62 wickets and Seagrams 60. The thing was poised; the match was against Penrith. The Trogs batted first. It was Jonty and Seagrams' turn to open the batting. Almost at once Seagrams called a run, cancelled it when Jonty was half way down the wicket, and ran him out. This ensured that Seagrams would win the batting award in the Tontine, no one else being nearer than Allerton with a total of 401. Jonty, so far from being indignant at Seagrams' foul behaviour, congratulated him warmly on his win and seemed very cool and comfortable. Surely there were currents moving beneath this smooth surface? Had Jonty, perhaps, some God-given assurance that his time too would come?

'When the Trogs took the field, two wickets fell before either Jonty or Seagrams was put on, which left eight wickets for them to reap as they could. Jonty got two of them with beastly flukes – a batsman falling on his wicket, and a horrid shooter. Then his eight overs were done. So Seagrams would need five wickets to gain the double event. Bowling at the other end, he had in fact achieved four of them (two stumpings, one chap bowled rather cleverly round his legs, and a seedy lbw) while Jonty took his two. When Jonty came off, Seagrams still had his eighth and final over to bowl. No wicket, and he would merely tie with Jonty for the second leg of the Tontine: one wicket and he would take all.

'He bowled five balls, which the batsmen played back to and hit quietly on the long hop for singles. But at his sixth ball the batsmen facing Seagrams was seized by a demon: he romped down the wicket, attempted a drive on the half-volley, found the ball with the meat of the bat, but was just too much underneath it. The ball soared slowly, like a tiny gas balloon: Jonty ran round the boundary to get beneath it but had a long distance to cover; he extended on arm, the ball fell plop into his cupped hand, he raised it above his head then stretched his arm towards Seagrams to salute his double victory in the Tontine, while the fir trees beyond the trout stream sent back the echo of our acclamation, acclamation less of Seagrams' triumph than of Jonty's superb, his English, chivalry.

'Seagrams glowed and preened. He had won Jonty body and soul.

'Then Jonty called to the umpires. "Come over here, please, gentlemen." Both umpires went, and so did I. "I have not moved my feet since I had the catch under proper control," says Jonty. Both feet were an inch the wrong side of the whitewashed boundary line. The umpires shook their heads. Jonty looked at Seagrams, slowly lowered his arm, dropped the ball in front of him.

'"No catch," he called to Seagrams. "Sorry, squire."

'Seagrams slumped like an empty skin.

'As captain of the Trogs,' JBB went on, 'I judged that Seagrams' behaviour in running Jonty out deliberately was

'Both feet were an inch the wrong side of the whitewashed boundary line'

so shitty that, whereas he must be allowed, on grounds of the actual figures, to keep the batting award of the Tontine, the bowling award should *not* be divided between them as for a tie but given in entirety to Jonty. What I did not know then, but only learned from Jonty years later, was that the catch was absolutely fair but Jonty had wriggled his feet back, while all eyes were on his raised arm, in order to snatch the yearned-for prize of total victory away from Seagrams even as he was beginning to relish it with his whole being.

'Well, Seagrams was so crippled by deprivation in the wake of glory, so angry with me for declaring the honours level, that he cancelled the Trogs' visit for the next year and indeed, as it turned out, forever. For Jonty, having been placed in trial by combat on an equal footing with Seagrams, could now slip his chain and leave for the South, where Oudenarde House had made him an offer. Then the Lord of the Isle collapsed indeed: the parents, seeing that Jonty's decent face under its fresh auburn hair had departed the island, realising, from the way in which the defeated Seagrams now snarled at one and all, that his former smiles had been only a mask, drawing their own and pretty well correct

179

conclusions, withdrew their children in squads. The following summer, Seagrams not only iterated his refusal to receive the Trogs at Lord of the Isle but would not even play with us elsewhere. He went on an Hellenic cruise with the last of the money he could scrape up: one morning he was not in his cabin, and no man on earth has seen him since.'

'I still do not understand,' said the Chancellor, 'why Jonty is in doubt about playing with us this summer.'

'Jonty has come to think that he killed Seagrams, first by tricking him over the Tontine and then by deserting the Lord of the Isle. Jonty says that every time he plays with the Trogs these days he feels, not exactly guilt, but a long, creeping sadness, when he thinks of the old times on the island and of Seagrams bowling (and whipping) in his prime.'

July 24, 1987, Selsted cricket ground by Canterbury

First day of the Trogs' Tour in Kent. The Selsted Match. O. Paradore and Lazarus Risen Plumb arrive promptly (O. apparently stone sober). Cannon next, sinewy as ever, proboscis twitching for dirt and trouble. The Chancellor is here too, says he has a full ten days' leave from his 'research', and has been firmly refused permission by JBB to bring his Lithuanian mistress. ('Cannon will cuckold him,' says JBB aside, 'and then there'll be a scene.')

O. recalls the first time he played for the Trogs: on this

ground in 1970, as a last minute substitute:–

'I'd come down to see Raven before leaving for Malaya. Then comes this call to the colours of the Trogs. Hadn't played cricket since an Army match at Brunswick, when it pissed with rain after the first over and we all went off to spend the afternoon in the medieval brothel-quarter – Ghibelline walls and a Gothic gate and women splaying in the windows. That was the time when Dick Cock was told by his whore to stop ploughing, just as he was warming up for the *coup d'arriver*, because the wireless played God Save the Queen on the BAOR network, and she said he must desist out of respect for Her Majesty. We all had to hang around forever while Dick got started up again, with beastly Red Caps liable to come prowling by at any moment. And that game of cricket, such as it was, had been in 1954, so you can imagine I didn't look forward to this affair in 1970 with much confidence – and the less confidence as I was fitted out with a pair of Raven's trousers three times too large round the waist and an old jockstrap so tight that it cut into my groin like a mantrap.'

'I remember you made some useful runs,' says JBB.

O. Paradore's tale of the Selsted match (1970)

And you know why? (O. continues his tale.)

I simply had to stay at the wicket. Your boy, James, still in his dear little knickers in those days, was watching the match with his mother, when who should join them but my uncle Giles, who used to live in Folkestone and often came to Trog matches in Kent (so I discovered later). But the thing was, at the time I hadn't the faintest idea that uncle G. might turn up, and I'd never have played had I known, because my horrible old mother thought I'd already gone to Malaya, and if she'd realised I was playing hookey in Kent instead of spending my whole embarkation leave, right down to the last dregs of it, sucking up to her in London, she'd probably have changed her will and shot me down to the bottom of the ladder. So far, as the eldest child, I was precariously clinging to the top, and there with any luck I would stay all the time I was abroad (out of sight, out of trouble) *providing* that I got clear of England without a row; and by the time I got back she damn well ought to be in her box. Now then: if Uncle Giles saw me, he was going to tell my mother, and the next thing one knew she'd go whingeing off to the law men and Uncle Giles would be ladling my notes out of the family chest when Mummy bit the dust. So it was vital Uncle G. shouldn't know I was there. Luckily a wicket fell just before he arrived, and I'd gone in to bat, so at least he couldn't meet me on the boundary. On the other hand I might be even more conspicuous in the middle. But yet again, Uncle G. had pretty bad sight, as a result of sixty years' addiction to deep brown juice, and he didn't associate me with cricket. So I persuaded one of the fieldsmen to lend me a great floppy panama he was wearing and more or less

hid hull down under that. And there I managed to stay, prodding and poking; but still Uncle Giles didn't budge, nor would do, I realised, till the pub opposite the ground opened up, which wouldn't be until six. It was now half-past five, and try as I might someone was going to send my bails spinning before half an hour was up, and then I should have to walk, straight past James and his mother and Uncle Giles, in order to get to the pavilion.

So what was a fellow to do? Luckily James had to be sent off to the lav just then, and this made Uncle Giles mindful of his own leaky bladder, so he decided to go for a squirt too. And as I saw him totter into the gents I knew I had at least five minutes to get away from the wicket and hide, because the last time I had had a pee with Uncle Giles in his club it took him at least three minutes to get the old pipe clear and flowing (or rather, dribbling) and another three to check all the drops off. So I opened my shoulders, hoping to get out there and then, and simply succeeded in hitting a sequence of sixes – useful runs as JBB remarked so kindly just now, but quite beside my present purpose. However, at last I did hole out on the long-on boundary, and scuttled away, in order to be safely hidden in the changing room by the time Uncle G. came out of the pisser, which must be at any second now. But just as I sat down under my peg and congratulated myself on my escape, and started working out that Uncle G. would be departing for the public in just under twenty minutes and once there would not be seen again and then everything could go on as normal – just as I was mulling all that over in my brainbox, I suddenly realised that I myself wanted to pee, and pee like a dray horse at that. The excitement of batting had disguised the need but now – now go I must or burst asunder.

In those days, friends, there was on this ground one gents and only one – the one in which Uncle Giles was still tediously draining his awful old snake. There I could not go, or the game would have been U.P. Now that I was delivered, now that I was so near to sanctuary – actually in it, in fact – I was determined not to give myself up to Uncle G. But where to piddle? For piddle I must. Out of the window, I thought. I stood on a bench, yanked open the only window there was – high up in the wall, more like a ventilator – and sent a fine parabola of steaming peewee arching up through the opening, spattering the glass a bit, but most of it curving elegantly down and away, as smooth as a rural rivulet in a poem by Pope. Then, *'Zounds!'* came from the other side of the window, *'Gadzooks and Hellfire!'*

At first I thought I'd sprayed a pair of country copulatives who might be sporting behind the pav; but then I worked out that country copulatives don't usually use Elizabethan expletives. Nor was any female protest (as might be, 'It's ruined my perm what cost me three-and-sixpence') associated with the male one. And then I remembered, too, that Uncle

184

Giles was much given, in his few sober hours on earth, to reading Elizabethan and Jacobean dramas (he liked the bits in which people were disembowelled or slowly chopped up piecemeal), and when I heard the voice continue, 'A Welsh pox on it. God's Death, but I've been soused like a rotten herring in a nun's closet,' together with other rather oddly mixed images, I realised what had happened.

I crept into the main body of the pavilion. James came grinning in and told the company:

'There was a funny old friend of Mummy's sitting with us. I had to go for a weewee, so he came too; and when I'd finished he was still doing it, so I thought it would be polite to wait for him outside. When at last he came out, we walked back behind the pavvy to where Mummy was sitting, and suddenly a great shower of bright yellow widdle came out of a high-up window and landed on the old gentleman's head. I wanted to laugh but that would have been rude. He smelt so awful he's had to go away.'

July 1987, Selsted cricket ground by Canterbury

'So there,' concludes O., 'is my last memory of this ground – seventeen years ago. Funny thing, you know: in those days I was absolutely parafit and as keen as curry. I'd had my setbacks, of course, failed to get into Staff College for one;

185

but I was still devoted to the Army and longing to be out in Malaya. Yet from that time on everything started to go downhill. I was promised promotion to substantive Lieutenant-Colonel if I agreed to guarantee five years more service, and as soon as I'd signed the guarantee they cancelled even my temporary and local Colonelcy and pulled me back to Major – sorry, they said, but establishments were being reduced all round. Then I was promised I could call myself "Colonel" when I finally retired, and so I do (for what it's worth), but they tried to rat on that deal too. They said it was no longer policy to allow ex-officers to call themselves by a rank higher than they had *substantively* attained. Luckily I'd made *them* sign a piece of paper promising the honorary rank. Of course they'd "lost" it when it came to the point, but I'd taken ten photocopies and kept feeding these in each time they "lost" another.

'"I'll make five hundred more, if need be," I told them. Then they said that photocopies didn't count (new security regulation) ... and produced chapter and verse. But luckily a Corporal Clerk, who owed me for a good turn from way back, found the original and passed it on to me.

'"There you are," I said, showing it to them but holding it tight by both ends, "Your promise." So they gave in, but not before they'd nearly ground their dentures into powder.'

'What had you done,' enquired the Chancellor, 'to make them so hostile?'

'God knows.'

'*I* know,' said Lazarus Risen Plumb, 'that is, if your form stayed the same as it was when I was soldiering with you.'

Everyone looked at Plumb with interest.

'For many years before we retired,' Plumb said, 'Colonel Paradore and myself were serving in different regiments. He went parachuting, while I stayed with the Light Infantry. But in the old days' – his face glowed slightly – 'for the first

186

six years or so after O. was commissioned and before he got the parachute bug, we were very much together. What made all senior officers loathe and mistrust O., what made them determined to do him down if they could, was his capacity for injurious jokes.'

JBB won the toss: the Trogs were to bat: the afternoon murmured and drowsed around us while we were drawn easily into the whirligig of reminiscence.

July 1987, Selsted, Major Plumb's tale of Colonel Paradore's military indiscretions

They came so naturally to him, these jokes (continued Plumb), that he didn't even know he was making them – and countless enemies with them. There was the business of Major Phillips. With the old 99th Light Infantry in the Harz. Of course I was a Serjeant then so I didn't know at first-hand what went on in the Officers' Mess. But an officer called Captain Halberd (a side glance at O.) used to tell me quite a lot. Apparently this Major Paddy Phillips was passionately or at least persistently in love with one of the WVS ladies who came out from England to run canteens and entertainments for the soldiery, in the hope that they would stay in barracks instead of going out and catching the clap. Major Phillips' lady was a rugged but fetching number (for her years) called Hilda. O. would watch until he'd seen

Paddy Phillips go into the bathroom and heard him turn on the taps. Then he'd poke his swede round the door and say, 'Hilda's on the phone.' Paddy would turn off the taps and go to the telephone – two floors up. The phone would be dead. While he was going and coming back, O. would switch the lever from 'Taps' to 'Shower': Paddy Phillips wouldn't notice this had been done, turn on the taps again – only to get a drenching from a hissing and writhing shower apparatus on his best Paisley dressing gown. At this stage some subaltern that O. has arranged comes in and says, 'Hilda on the phone, Paddy. Something the matter with the line last time she tried.' So off Paddy plonks again, up two floors, picks up the phone and hears a voice say,

'There was a young lady called Hilda
Who did what her fiancé willed her.
　　Now he was called Paddy
　　And looked like her Daddy,
A thing that indecently thrilled her.'

Down went the receiver with a snort of disgust, back went Paddy to the bathroom, remembered that he had left the lever on 'Shower', switches it back to 'Taps' (or so he thinks), and gets another drenching as someone has already switched it in his absence. And so on.

'What happened about their marriage?' asks O. 'I was gone by the time it came off.'

'It was very happy,' returns Plumb, 'until Paddy died after a year of it. Another instructive example of how the gods grudge human felicity.'

'The gods? Or God?' enquires James. And does not stay for an answer. 'You know,' he says to O., 'I remember that business of your Uncle Giles in 1970 – though of course at that time I didn't know who he was, I just thought he was

someone of my mother's. Ghastly performance he put on in
the gents. He had to jump up and down before he could
start peeing, then whistle "Cockles and Mussels" to keep it
coming, and God (or the gods) know what. What happened
to him?'

'Died not long after. What else? I should have known that
an old soak like him was no very serious candidate for
favours in my mother's will. She was an abstainer – the
miserable old sow. Oddly enough, Uncle G. left me his
collection of sixteenth- and seventeenth-century plays. It
made my mother frantic with jealousy – though she never
read a book and was pretty well illiterate.'

'But of course that affair of Paddy Phillips,' resumes Plumb
to all of us, 'was only the tip of the iceberg. Some of O.'s
tricks were so appalling that I do not dare relate them to
comparative strangers.'

'Then let me relate one,' says the Chancellor. 'You didn't know then,' he said to O., 'or indeed until now, that your name was in fact familiar to me twenty-five years ago. When you were taking the Staff College examinations. If you remember, you got enough marks in aggregate to procure your immediate entry into Staff College, regardless of commanding officers' reports and so on, or of anything that any of your enemies could possibly say or do.'

'I remember very well,' says O. 'The only trouble was that in one paper I scored only 49% – and under 50% in any paper automatically failed a candidate no matter how high his score overall.'

'Thereby lies this tale,' the Chancellor says.

The Chancellor's tale of O.'s further military indiscretions (Cheltenham 1962)

It was while I was working in one of our special departments in Cheltenham, (the Chancellor pursues). One morning a bowler-hatted bugger sidles in and says, 'Special job for you.'

'Oh yes,' I says, 'and who might you be?'

'Military security,' he croaks; and shows his card.

'Military security,' I tell him, 'is not my game.'

'We need your help.'

He then explains that there is an officer called Major O.

Paradore, formerly of the 99th Light Infantry but presently attached to a holding unit at Hinckly Aerodrome near Oxford for parachute training. It appears that this Paradore chappie has just been sitting the Staff College Examination, that although the marks have not yet been officially published he is known to have achieved an overall mark of something higher than 90%, and according to all Queen's rules and regs he must be admitted to the Staff College at Camberley with the very next intake, i.e. in about three months' time, and that nothing whatever can be done to stop this, since such a splendid result qualifies him for immediate or special entry.

'And quite right too,' I tell him.

'Not if he is a security risk,' says my visitor.

'And is he?'

'Well, as far as we know, Paradore is not exactly a *security* risk, but his behaviour and opinions are ... let us say ... subversive.'

'Subversive of what? Good order and military discipline?'

'Well, no, not quite that. Subversive of ... respect. Not just respect for his senior officers but respect for *all* the things an officer ought to respect.'

'Like the Queen?' I enquire.

Well, no, as far as that went Major Paradore was known to be an adequately loyal officer. The sort of respect he subverted was respect for ... well ... marriage, the family, religion, the old school tie ...

'You're just trying to tell me,' I remark, in none too friendly a tone, 'that his face doesn't fit. That's why they have this system of special entry, you know: so that if a fellow's got brains, which the Army most urgently needs, he can't be shoved off the gravy train by you and your sort just because his face don't fit.'

By this time (continues the Chancellor) my visitor was

191

getting rather desperate.

'Look,' he says, 'we have reason to suppose you can help us.'

'How?'

He's just opening his cakehole to tell me when I stop him and say, 'First of all give me one good reason why I should.'

All right. He would tell me a story to illustrate the diabolic quality of Paradore's subversiveness. And here it is:–

The Chancellor's visitor's tale of O.'s further military indiscretions, Her Majesty's troopship *Vulcan*, (late summer 1955)

When the 99th Light Infantry had been sailing to Mombasa on Her Majesty's troopship *Vulcan* some seven years before (deposed the Chancellor's visitor to the Chancellor) it was decreed that they should learn Swahili, a useful way of filling in the time. A clever chap was needed to instruct them and the choice fell on Major Paradore. But, Major Paradore had said, I do not know any Swahili. No more did anyone else on the boat, he was told; but there was, in *Vulcan*'s library, an ancient Swahili grammar which would do to be going on with. Let Major Paradore apply himself to this and then instruct his brother officers, keeping a step ahead of them.

Now, what Paradore's CO did not know was that Paradore had with him in his cabin an elementary *modern* Swahili

192

concordance and syntax, which he had brought along with him, being a forward-looking chap and rightly reckoning that when he reached Kenya a spot of Swahili might come in handy. However, this was the last thing he was going to tell the CO: first, because he resented being landed with an annoying job, secondly because he didn't want his nice new expensive Swahili book to be commandeered for the common weal – which was just the sort of thing the new, lean, mean CO would have done with it – and handed round from sweaty palm to sweaty palm, sneezed at and dribbled on and drink-bespattered, and have the odd chapter torn out by someone who found himself in the bog without a roll.

So Paradore went to the ship's library, and took out the ancient Swahili grammar. He then compared it with his spick and span concordance and made an amusing discovery. In Swahili, as in most languages, (a) an individual word can be used to convey many different meanings, the precise one intended depending either on the context or on the syn-tactical construction adopted; and (b) a number of harmless words, when altered by so much as a single letter, become vulgar, obscene or even explosive. Thus, in English, a 'cure' becomes a 'curse' or a 'cur' with no trouble at all, a 'harp' soon makes a 'harpy' or a 'pole' a 'prole'. This much, of course, is commonplace: the special interest for Paradore lay in the fact that Swahili is particularly rich in such broad shifts caused by tiny alterations and there are possibilities of ludicrous misunderstandings. Thus the simple remark that 'we are the only people here' can easily be taken to mean, if rendered in Swahili with a certain intonation, 'we are here for indecent purposes'.

So Paradore compiled a word list from the old Swahili book, which he had printed off on the ship's duplicator and distributed to all officers, warrant officers and serjeants in the 99th Light Infantry. A really careful comparison of the word list with the grammar would have revealed that occasional vowels were altered or consonants transposed, all venial errors in the tyro which O. was supposed to be, had it not been that these errors were perpetrated only after O.'s prolonged and detailed study of his own secret and far more comprehensive concordance. He also composed a list of elementary constructions, this time entirely accurate word by word and phrase by phrase, but which he knew, from a perusal of the modern book, were hideous in their import if used with the corrupt words he had provided in his word list.

He then proceeded to set his class an elementary prose. The English which was to be done into Swahili read as follows:—

In order to march with his battalion through the forest, the Colonel set his compass due west. This would bring him and the battalion out of the trees and on to the muddy shore of a lake at its northernmost point, provided they marched accurately on the bearing.

If the class diligently applied the entirely correct constructions in the second list which Paradore had issued to the subtly falsified vocabulary in the first, their proses would convey the following meaning in Swahili:

In order to inspect the genitals of the men in his battalion, the Colonel ordered a naked parade. He then exposed his own member and demonstrated to the battalion that, if rubbed with vigour, this part of the anatomy soon becomes stiff and can be inserted, with great pleasure, in the rectum of another male.

Paradore collected up the finished proses and a day or two later he informed the Adjutant that some of these compositions, including his own and the CO's, were of an excellence that demanded wider recognition. He proposed, if he might, to send them by Air Mail from Aden (where the ship must soon dock for twenty-four hours) to the educational section of Corps HQ in Nairobi, so that the officer i/c African Language Studies (and ultimately the General himself) might know how diligently and with what success the 99th 'were getting on with the job' (a favourite expression of the lean, mean CO) of learning Swahili on the voyage.

'And so it had come about,' the Chancellor told us on Selsted cricket ground, 'if my military visitor in Cheltenham was to be believed (and I for one reckon he was), that the Lieutenant-Colonel i/c African Language Studies in Nairobi received some pieces of Swahili by prominent field officers of the 99th, all of them on the same basic and abominable theme, with occasional minor variations caused by faulty use of Paradore's vocab. and syntax sheets. The Lieutenant-Colonel took the proses to the Colonel i/c Education, who took them to the Chief of Staff, who happened to be a gentleman and so, when the meaning was explained to him, laughed heartily and wrote a personal note to the CO of the 99th, which he received on arrival in Mombasa. This note congratulated the lean, mean CO on his command of the vernacular, with a jocular PS to the effect that the behaviour prescribed would be as good a way as any of keeping down the VD rate of the 99th while in a notoriously infected country. The puzzled CO called, as soon as he was in Nairobi, on the Lieutenant-Colonel i/c African Language Studies to request an explanation – and was given it. Whereupon he realised that he had somehow been tricked by Major Paradore and was very angry. As the event had turned out, the whole thing had been laughed off by an upper-class and highly eccentric Major-General, whose only interest in the

195

campaign in Kenya was the opportunity to collect rare butterflies in the White Highlands. But the CO's "prose" might well have landed on a very different desk with a very different result. In any case, the story would go the rounds and there would be much smirking at his expense.

'Paradore, summoned to the CO's office, wore a look of offended innocence. Having "borrowed" the old Swahili book from the *Vulcan*'s library in case of some such crisis, he was able to demonstrate to the CO that the words presented in his handout and subsequently used in the "proses" had indeed been culled from this source; and as for the occasional errors (tiny transpositions and misplaced vowels) in their reproduction – well, what could the Colonel expect if he commanded someone totally ignorant of the lingo to buff up on it and start giving lectures at twenty-four hours' notice? And of course many of the errors could have been due to mistakes by the clerk (even more ignorant of the tongue than Paradore) who typed the list on to the special "flimsy" required for use in the duplicator.

'And so,' says the Chancellor, 'let us return to the chappie who told me the story that morning in Cheltenham. Paradore, he said, had of course escaped without penalty; and equally, of course, everyone knew pretty well what had happened and there was much malicious merriment. But there was also a feeling that this kind of thing wouldn't quite do – a feeling that got stronger and stronger the higher it was held. Oh yes: "subversive" was the word. Subversion came under security if it came under anything: let security look to it. So here he was, looking at it: on no account must Major O. Paradore, the putative parachutist, formerly of the 99th Light Infantry, be allowed through the pearly gates of Staff College.

' "Well," I said to my visitor – Stoggins, he was called – "even if I were in agreement with you, what do you imagine

196

that I, a humble civil servant, could possibly do for you ... and how?"

' "You are known to have contacts," said Stoggins. "If one of your contacts were to inform you that an officer called Paradore is suspected – 'suspected' would be quite enough – of possibly having undesirable friends in a certain embassy, that would do the trick. Such a threat to security, no matter how vague and imprecise, would enable us to keep Paradore out of Staff College: talk of 'subversion' will not."

' "None of my contacts has ever mentioned a Major Paradore."

' "Are you *quite* sure?"

' "Yes."

' "If you search your conscience, don't you think you *might* find that someone, in the distant past, *might* just have mentioned the name Paradore or something near it?"

' "If I search my conscience, I know damn well that I never heard the name Paradore until you came into this office half an hour ago, and further that I consider him to be a splendid fellow to whom I wish the best of subversive luck."

'So off went Mr. Stoggins. One can only suppose,' said the Chancellor to O., 'that some bright spark in the Warhouse hit on the scheme of cooking your marks later. After all, no list had yet been published – perhaps it hadn't even been printed – when Stoggins came to see me in Cheltenham. Had you any weak subject in which they might have marked you down?'

'The paper in which I was marked at 49%,' said O., 'was Administration. Personally, I never was much of an administrator – all too boring – but I know the *theory* of the thing backwards.'

'Then can you think of any reason why you should have been penalised over your marks in that paper?'

O sighed. 'I'm afraid I did make one or two little jokes,' he said. 'I couldn't resist them.'

'What sort of jokes?' said Lazarus Plumb.

'I told that joke of Wellington's about the officer who slept with the regimental laundry woman and got poxed. "Serve the fellow right," said the Duke. "Even her mangle had the pox after my lord Tadcaster's breeches had been through it."'

'You might have known they couldn't stand jokes about VD. The official attitude is total pecksniffery.'

'I suppose so. But if it was all right for Wellington –'

'– Wellington was a Field Marshal when he cut that joke. What other gems did you put in?'

'One about the chain of command. I said the Queen was the titular fairy at the top of the Christmas Tree, but the real decisions were taken by the General Staff and the Army Council, to whom Her Majesty was constrained to condescend like Titania to the Ass.'

'Well. We can see why you only got 49% for Administration.'

'But the point is,' said O., 'that according to the Chancellor here I originally had enough marks in that too. It must have been later, between that chap's coming to see him and the publication of the official results, that they did me down. I wonder who thought of *that*?'

'Somebody or other whose pisser you'd been pulling too long and too hard in the hurly burly,' said Lazarus Plumb. 'Never you mind, O. It's too late to bother now.'

JBB went in to bat and came out two balls later.

'Just the same way as I was out at Lord of the Isle in 1967,' JBB told us, 'slanting the bat to hit the ball over square leg and then making a miscue.'

'Slanting the bat is a dangerous proceeding,' remarked James.

'I've often got away with it. But today, like that time at
the Lord of the Isle, it went wrong. For the same reason.
Legs.'

'You mean ... you got yourself in the wrong position?
Badly balanced?'

'No. Other people's legs. I caught a glimpse. On the
boundary. Seventeen-year-old legs, bare and brown, under
a very short skirt. A distraction, you understand, marring
one's judgment and making one apply the wrong slant to
one's bat. Today the legs belonged to that girl over there by
the scoreboard. At Lord of the Isle they belonged to a girl
who'd come to take care of James for the afternoon – he
was still in nappies then – while his mother went shopping
on the mainland.'

'You mean,' said James, 'that you *leched* after my nanny?'

JBB's tale of the Lord of the Isle (August 1967)

'Only theoretically,' pleaded JBB, 'and only for five seconds. But long enough to be punished. God found me out. My own hankering found me out, causing me to slant my bat until it was almost horizontal and to spoon the ball into the hands of short leg instead of sending it soaring over the boundary. I'll tell you another thing,' said JBB. 'I wasn't the only person to notice that girl's legs, that day at Lord of the Isle. All those lustful brutes that had come to play against us from Carlisle – Stroppington and Jimmie and Busker and Izzy the Ice Cream Man – they all spotted her and got instant hots for her the moment she started wheeling James along the boundary in his pushchair. Dindyma, she was called, daughter of a forester from Windermere, and lovely like a water nymph, long and wriggly with back hair down to her buttocks and tiny little tits like racquet balls –'

'Steady, father,' said James. 'I know the insurance is all in order, but we don't want to lose you just yet.'

'When I'd got over my annoyance at being out,' JBB said, 'I began to think what was best to do. Stroppington and Jimmie and the rest, who were playing, as I told you, for Carlisle, were in the field and were going to have to stay there until the end of the Trogs' innings. Obvious thing to do: tell Dindyma to whisk herself and the infant James away as soon as the eighth wicket fell. So I went for a word with Dindyma, who was fondling lucky James in her lap.

'"Look, Dindyma," I said, "this is rather embarrassing, but I have to tell you that some of the chaps from Carlisle have an eye for a lovely girl like you and will stop at nothing – nothing, Dindyma – to have their wicked way."

'"Oh," says she, coaxing her satin thighs out of her dress

till I can see her frillies, "and what way is that? Doodle doodle," she says to James and scratches his bottom very lightly with her finger nails. ("More, more," gurgles James, and gets it.)

'"Look," I tell her, "I don't want to make a drama out of this, but it will be in everyone's best interest if you take James back into the school and up to my room – we've been given the Blue Chamber in the South Wing – and lock the door and stay there until either my wife or I arrives on the scene later."

'"You want me to go now?"

'"When eight of our wickets are down. Before the Carlisle fellows come off the field."

'"But Mrs. Budden said that James and I were to stay here. 'Stay near the pavilion until I come,' she said. 'On no account move. Talk to nobody except my husband, particularly not to Mr. Seagrams, and wait for me to come.'"

'"I think she was thinking much the same as me," I told her. "It's just that her instructions are a little different because she didn't know quite how – er – animated the scene might become."

'"Anyhow," says Dindyma, "Mrs. Budden has taken the key of your room with her, so unless you have one yourself, James and I will have to stay here."

'And with that she falls to tickling James on his little rump again. And of course I haven't got my key with me. So of course she's got to stay there by the pavilion.

'"All right," I command, "stay here. But don't leave that child for a single second." For James, I thought, was a better chaperone than none.

'Meanwhile, the Trogs were getting restless. Although I was mainly concerned about the Carlisle men, the Trogs were by no means all slouches in this field. Seagrams, our host and Headmaster of Lord of the Isle, could be very

201

flamboyant; Jonty Delaware could draw a good bow; Cannon was not so named for nothing; Davy Strutt could turn a neat phrase; Odo Warrington had a pretty face and a trim calf; and so on. All these and more, many of whom had seen Dindyma around before and taken a fancy, now sat down on the grass in a discreet circle of about four yards radius with Dindyma and James at its centre. Desultory remarks were passed. Dindyma, obeying her orders, absolutely ignored everybody except James, whom she was now entertaining with some new game, to the sweaty envy of the Trogs, to say nothing of Izzy the Ice Cream Man and the rest of the fieldsmen.

'"Couchy-couchy-coo," trilled Dindyma, rubbing James's face and chest first on one racquet-ball tit and then on the other ... Well, I thought, there's safety in numbers. Nothing is going to happen as long as she is surrounded by eight Trogs, smoulder as they may. And I walked up the lawn to make a telephone call in the school, turning at every terrace to confirm that decorum still obtained by the pavilion.

'When I came out ten minutes later, the scene had changed. Dindyma had now replaced James, who was apparently asleep, in his pushchair, and was pushing him slowly round the boundary, under the trees, away towards the trout stream. The eight infatuated Trogs, headed by Seagrams, were slowly following in Indian file, at intervals of about ten feet. Very ridiculous they looked. I wonder, I thought, why she's disobeyed her orders, which were to stay absolutely still by the pavilion until my wife Jackie came to her. Still, I thought, there's no harm she can come to, what with James and eight almost contiguous Trogs; the trees this side of the stream aren't quite thick enough on the ground to provide cover for any kind of *amour*; and while the copse on the other side could conceal an orgy of battalion strength, there is no way one can get across to it, without going nearly a mile to the shore of the island, where there is a footbridge.

'Then came trouble. That well-known phenomenon, a Trog batting collapse, began. This rapidly removed four figures in the queue behind Dindyma, all of whom had to hurry back to the pavilion and put their pads on. But the other four in the queue had all batted and been out. Seagrams and Jonty Delaware were first in the pursuit, followed by two total no-hopers (as we thought), a spotty boy called Birch, from Stowe, and a tiny Indian undergraduate from Oxford, said to be a brilliant mathematician and known to be a competent bowler of googlies, but so ill-favoured, with no chin and horizontally jutting teeth, that his starting price must be at least 150 to 1.

'Round the boundary they all proceeded. They turned back from the trout stream and approached the terraced lawn. Good, I thought: she's coming back to the pav. Who can blame her if she wanted a bit of a stroll? But no. When she reached the point at which she should have turned right from the bottom of the lawn towards the pavilion, she continued straight on until she came to the steps that led up to the first terrace. All four aspirants leapt forward to offer help with James's pushchair. Dindyma, still totally silent, pointed to Seagrams and Jonty. Between them they carried the chair, James still asleep inside it, up the stone steps to the first terrace. Dindyma stood at the bottom. She removed her dress, revealing a tenuous bikini arrangement, and handed it to Birch, indicating that he and the Indian should now follow her as she walked up towards the first terrace and imperiously gestured to Jonty and Seagrams to lift the chair up the second flight. And then up the third and last, Birch with her dress and the Indian, as yet the only unencumbered male of the party, still following. When they all came to the top level, Dindyma turned, stretched out her arms as though to embrace the entire cricket field and all the gawping Carlisleans on it, stripped off the top section of her bikini, revealed her two racquet balls, wriggled until they bounced up and down on her breastbone, handed the garment to the Indian, and vanished through the glass door into the school.

'Eager as I was to rush up there and discipline the entire group, I was at this point engaged by the scorers as arbiter of a complicated squabble to do with the recording of No Balls. When I had resolved this I started towards the terrace – only to see the entire procession come down again, in reverse order, with Dindyma, now fully clad once more, marching to one side, rather like a section commander.

'Birch and the Indian were the first to reach me.

' "What on earth – "

' "She wanted to go to the loo," said Birch. "She left her kit and young James outside with us, had a pee like a warhorse for all of four minutes, then came out, put on her ... things ... again, and ordered us, by hand, to proceed back down the steps."

'By then Seagrams and Jonty had come sweating down with the pram. They put it down, Dindyma took it over, James woke up and started squealing, Dindyma leant forward and quieted him with some efficacious intimacy, and then turned to me.

' "Here is your son back," she said to me. "I'm sorry I had to move but I had to go to the toilet."

' "Loo," I said.

' "What?"

' "Oh, nothing. Why such a production?"

' "There is no toilet in the pavilion. I'd hoped to pop into the trees, but they weren't nearly thick enough and all those men were following. So I had to go up to the school; and I had to get James up there with me. How else could I have managed it?"

204

' "But why," I said, "why all that performance with your dress? And your bikini?"

' "I had to take my dress off because I hate rucking it up."

' "But why take it off in public?"

' "The ladies' toilets in Mr. Seagrams' school are filthy, even though there are at this time contractors hired to clean them, and there is, in any case, not room to take off a dress inside the cubicles."

' "All right. But Dindyma" – here, surely, I had her – "why did you remove your brassière and exhibit yourself in view of the entire island?"

' "To make a scandal. Before night someone will tell my father. He will beat me. But at last he will now let me leave here and go to the London School of Economics this autumn. I have a place. He says I cannot go to London so young. I shall now tell him that until he gives his permission I shall do as I did today, I shall wave my breasts about – and worse – all round the island, all round Windermere, Keswick, Penrith, even Carlisle. For very shame he must surrender. He will give me a final beating, which I shall not much mind as he is a manly man, behaving as such a man should to a daughter who is being a slut; and then he will let me go. It is the only way. Come, Jamie darling, we shall go and sit beside the pavilion, till Mrs. Budden comes, and make little games with one another."

'Squeaks of eager anticipation.

' "What shall you do," I said, "if those fellows from Carlisle come sniffing round you later on?"

' "Your son will defend me."

' "I don't quite see – "

' " – He was overexcited not long ago and I must now change his diaper. The one he is wearing, when removed, will make a good weapon against any daft crud of them all that may come near me." '

205

S.R. now continues the account of what happened
after the Carlisle match at the Lord of the Isle on
August 20, 1967

(S.R.'s diary.) Carlisle had won, I remember, on the day of
Dindyma's strip (as it was always subsequently known) and
were dined up at the school. Jackie Budden, replacing the
caterer's chef (drunk), cooked superbly, Jimmie sang (about
the last song he ever sang, though then we could not know
it), Seagrams provided Burgundies and port worthy of the
occasion and of his own generosity (for this was long before
the bad days began at the Lord of the Isle), the moon shone
upon the terraced lawn and one hoped that life would last
for ever.

The tone of the evening went briefly awry when Izzy the
Ice Cream Man suggested to Seagrams that the school give
him a contract for soft drinks.

'That's all taken care of by the caterers.'

'I don't mean now, squire. I wouldn't be found dead
drinking my own soft drinks. I mean when the boys and
girls come back in September.'

'What's in it for me?' says Seagrams.

'Money.'

'And for my pupils?'

'Drinks which make them ever more thirsty: so that they
can go on drinking forever. Pleasure that can never cloy;
and appetite that doth increase by feeding.'

'Explain.'

'My soft drinks,' says Izzy, 'include a certain quantity of
a specially treated sugar which, after a short while, makes
the drinker even more thirsty than he was before. Thus the
consumer goes through the bliss of slaking his thirst with a

long, cool draft, only to find that his desire for such delicious drafts is greater than ever.'

'A pity,' remarks Seagrams, 'that nobody knows how to apply a similar ingredient to sex. Just think how marvellous – a bloody great orgasm, followed, in a few moments, by an ever fiercer erection than the last.'

'It would very soon kill you,' I say.

'And that,' says Jonty, 'is pretty well what Izzy's soft drinks would do for you. They'd either make you sick your stomach out or increase the body's sugar content so swiftly and violently that you'd end up with terminal diabetes.'

'Look,' says Izzy, 'I'm not promoting a get-fit campaign; I'm trying to make money for me and happiness for my customers. A list of the ingredients in my soft drinks is to be found on the label on the bottle, in accordance with the law of the land. If neither the Consumer Council nor the Ministry of Health (or whatever it calls itself nowadays) have any complaints to make, then why should you have?'

'Do they know about the specially treated sugar?'

'They know what it's mixed with, yes. An ordinary colourant. The fact that the colourant, mixed with sugar, makes people thirsty,' said Izzy, 'is my discovery. By mistake I spilt a gallon or two into the brew I was making for Whitsun a couple of years back. I tested the brew to see if it tasted right. More sugar now needed. So I puts in more sugar and tastes it again, and find I have to rush to the sink for a pint of honest water. Then I work out a ratio of sugar to colourant for the rest of the brew that won't act quite so dramatically. I don't want a stampede at my soft drinks stall, just steady custom. And I get it. Now then, squire: do you want to sign a contract with me to provide a standing order of my soft drinks for your school, or don't you? I'll knock twenty per cent off the usual cost price, since it's you, and you can charge your pupils or their dads a bit below the normal selling price and tell them how generous you're being, when all the time you'll be quids in. Now what about it?'

'I'll think about it, Izzy,' says Seagrams. 'What about a deal on ice cream as well? They eat a lot of that in the summer.'

Izzy shudders.

'Not my ice cream,' he says. 'My soft drinks I'll sell to you because I've got to make a living, but my ice cream is definitely not for nicely nurtured kiddies. Strictly for Scousers, my ice cream. For sale in Liverpool only and in Blackpool if things are going rough.'

There was a yell from the window:

'*Lucrezia is coming!*'

From the window one could see a barge, rowed by six oarsmen on either bulwark, slowly approach the little quayside. Lucrezia Lippit, one of whose children had just left the Lord of the Isle with a Seagrams-style scholarship to Rugby, was sitting enthroned in the stern, got up as the Queen of Sheba; and around her was her court, Vitreus and Vanushka Clere-Story, Milesy Malbruges, Beatty Belhampton and Brigadier-General Pavey, all nearly twenty years younger than when we first encountered them in the early pages of this memoir, twenty years younger and twenty years more appetising, which in the case of Milesy Malbruges was not much to write home about but in the case of Lucrezia was enough to inflame a second millenium mummy.

Milesy, who had his backgammon set, at once engaged Izzy in a spot cash contest. Lucrezia, Vanushka and Beatty engaged the attention of Stroppington, Jimmie and Busker, who were now fortunately so drunk that they could offer only the most theoretical advances. Vity and the General took on Jonty and Seagrams at billiard fives, after which the General took JBB on one side to enquire for which regiment the infant James was intended. JBB said he proposed to postpone this decision for the next month or two, but the General, taking JBB by one arm and myself by the other, led us on to the terrace under the moon and said: –

'I entreat you not to delay. Did you ever hear the story of Barrington Yeats?'

No, we did not.

The Brigadier-General's tale

Barrington was born into a Coldstream family in 1918. He went to Sandhurst in the mid-'thirties with the absolute intention, which had long since been intimated to the regimental Lieutenant-Colonel in Birdcage Walk, of joining the family regiment as soon as he was commissioned. Everything nice and tidy, no hint of a problem anywhere ... until one morning Barrington gets a letter from a posh firm of solicitors which says that Barrington's Uncle Joshua has died of beri-beri or something of the sort in Kenya, having left Barrington twenty thousand notes on the nail and another ninety thou. in the funds. There was only one snag: if Barrington wanted to collect the loot when he came of age (it would be held in trust until then) he must take a commission, not in the Coldstream, but in the Cumbrian Fusiliers, Uncle Joshua's old regiment – the point being that Uncle Joshua had always been a bit of a bolshie and had joined the Fusiliers instead of the Guards simply to be annoying; and now he wanted Barrington to be annoying too.

Well, in 1937 twenty grand in grisbies was a fortune, let alone the ninety in shares. Barrington's branch of the family wasn't rich, and would indeed have quite a job to punt up the five hundred *per annum* which Barrington would need as an allowance in the Guards over and above his pay. One hundred and ten grand were not to be sniffed at. So they all thought of a clever wheeze. Barrington would apply for and accept a commission in the Cumbrian Fusiliers when he passed out from Sandhurst; he would grab the loot from Uncle J.'s lawyer when he was twenty-one, early in 1939; and then he'd apply to be transferred to the Coldstream. The regimental Lieutenant-Colonel of the Coldstream was discreetly approached by Barrington's Uncle Ledward; and when his embassage was coolly received, he was replaced by Barrington's Aunty Letty, who generated enough good will in Birdcage Walk and Albany to do the trick for Barrington.

Having squared the Coldstream, the family now had the problem of the Cumbrian Fusiliers. The trouble here was that Barrington's Uncle Joshua wasn't in the least popular in his old regiment. He'd spent most of the Boer War as ADC to an old chum of his father (Uncle Joshua cut a fine figure in overalls with his sword slung) and when the 1914 affair blew up he had just contrived, with characteristic forethought, to get himself appointed as military adviser to one of the more loathsome minor Indian princes. So that was two cushy wars on Uncle Joshua's record, to say nothing of his having taken large sums off several brother officers at piquet and having put horns on several more at Skindle's. What with all this (and a great deal more) it was far from certain that an application from Barrington to join the Cumbrian Fusiliers would be charitably entertained. Once again, however, Aunt Letty was wheeled into action; and again she did the trick (a trick she was very fond of) for her nephew Barrington, who was, of course, expected to show his gratitude in the appropriate manner. In later life Aunt Letty always used to say that Barrington had been the most versatile of all her lovers, having 'a right-angled piece like a tap which induced the most amazing sensations'; but that is another story.

So Barrington marched up the college steps and out of Sandhurst and into the Cumbrian Fusiliers and off to India, having first popped into Chancery Lane, collected Uncle J.'s legacy the moment it was ripe, and punted it into Cox and King's. In India his battalion was stationed at Bangalore: easy climate, easy duties, easy come (bored wives whose husbands were in the Plains), easy go (applications for local leave granted at a glance). But soon came another snag. According to the schedule, Barrington was to pay his Uncle Joshua Manes the courtesy of staying in the Cumbrian Fusiliers for half a year after collecting the old rotter's swag, and was then to apply for his transfer to the Coldstream. The half year was now up and Barrington must apply; his family wished it and so did he (truth to tell, the Cumbrian Fusiliers were a stuffy crowd in those days, which possibly explains why they had never appreciated Uncle Joshua) and so did the regimental Lieutenant-Colonel of the Coldstream, who had made all the necessary arrangements at Letty's passionate entreaty, and did not want his muster roll buggered up. So Barrington formed up to his CO in Bangalore and said his little piece: he was proud to have been accepted by the Fusiliers, and grateful for the experience he had gathered during his service with them, but now his old father was dying and had expressed a wish that Barrington should apply for a transfer to the Coldstream Guards (in which regiment his father had served during two wars and for twenty-five years) etc., etc., etc., and now could his formal request kindly be forwarded to the regimental Lieutenant-Colonel of the Coldstream Guards in Birdcage Walk, to the officer i/c Records, to the Horse Guards, etc., etc., etc.?

No, said Barrington's CO; it couldn't.

With respect, sir, why not?

Because this was July of 1939 and there was going to be a war in Europe. And just about everywhere else. Everything, said the CO unhappily (he was one of the jolly, pear-shaped, pre-war lot), was going to change. No more local leave. More training. No siestas. Preparations for forming subsidiary battalions of all regiments were already under way. Barrington was one of the corps of Cumbrian Fusilier officers who would assist in forming the new battalions in India or the Middle East from raw troops sent out for the purpose. 'It's all about as ghastly as it could be, dear boy,' wailed the pear-shaped Colonel, 'but what is a fellow to do? Your application must be refused.' Besides, added the Adjutant, who took a more martial view than his comfortable master, all berths in troopships were henceforth to be allotted on a basis of wartime priorities, and he took leave to opine that Barrington's transfer to the Guards' depot in Caterham would not be high among them.

Barrington was stuck. He later discovered that if he had applied but two weeks earlier, before his CO received a sheaf of special orders about putting things on a wartime footing, he would probably have been allowed his request. But that is by the way. All of Aunt Letty's caresses could not soothe the regimental Lieutenant-Colonel of the Coldstream, who vowed that never again would a Yeats be considered for the Coldstream or for anything else in the Brigade, if he could help it. It wasn't Barrington's fault, urged Aunt Letty, and started to tell the Lieutenant-Colonel about Barrington's taplike apparatus, in the hope of turning him on again or at least making him laugh. No good: Barrington was debarred from the Brigade for ever more.

'But surely, you will surmise,' said the General as we leaned over the parapet and listened to the distant murmuring of firs and chuckling of the trout stream, 'Barrington must have had a happy war in India, what with barra pegs and dhooli-bearers and syces and all those randy memsahibs. Not a bit of it. His newly formed battalion was stuffed with delinquents (who had volunteered at the outbreak of war to escape paying maintenance orders), it was twice sent to a punishment station, wiped out in Burma after some impossible demand from the fanatical Wingate, reformed in Calcutta (ugh) and finally despatched half way up the anus of the world, which, as you know, is the Persian Gulf. During Barrington's absence his money was badly invested by a dud stockbroker, and what was left was embezzled by a lawyer (to whom Barrington had given power of attorney) who was being blackmailed by another lawyer over just such another work of embezzlement.

'Barrington was killed in a Moslem riot because he was found to be uncircumcised. Possibly a merciful release.

'The point of this story is,' said the General, 'that over the choice of a regiment for one's son a decision must be made early and stuck to absolutely, no matter what inducements may come along in the form of money or what assistance may be mustered in the form of Aunt Letty. Had Barrington gone into the Coldstream straight from Sandhurst as originally planned he would have had a happy time of it: as it was he had a wretched life and a squalid death.'

'Even in the Coldstream things might have gone wrong for him,' I suggested.

'At least,' said the General, 'he would have had the consolation of knowing that he was in a proper regiment and not one of those regional showers-full of sheep-shagging nutters.'

Lord of the Isle (August 20, 1967)

(S.R.'s diary continued.) Beatty appeared on the terrace. 'I could kill filthy Seagrams,' she said. Beatty was at this time twenty-one and could cram all the puritan indignation of outraged youth and comeliness into sizzling fury. 'Do you know what he did?'

'No we don't. We can't imagine.' (Though we could and did – wrongly as it turned out.)

'Well. I wanted a piddle something fierce and found the girls' loo in a pretty bad way. I thought bloody Seagrams had this place especially purified for the Trogs, but I suppose there aren't enough female Trogs for anyone to worry about the ladies. So I hunted about upstairs and eventually found a pretty decent bathroom, loo and bidet and all. I locked the door and down I sat to let it rip, when suddenly a ladder crashes against the window and up comes Seagrams (he must have seen me go in) and leers and goggles through the window, which wasn't properly fastened, as he very soon noticed. So I think of getting over there to fasten it, but what the hell, waddling along with my knickers round my knees and still slashing like coot. So I just sit. And that

214

bastard Seagrams, he gets the window wide open, climbs in, prances across the floor, bows like a head waiter, says "May I have the honour?", and out with his thing and pisses straight down between my thighs, just twitching my bush. At least he's accurate, I'll say that.

' "What the devil are you doing?" I shout.

' "This is my bathroom, madam, my private bathroom, and therefore my lav, and if I want to pee in it I will."

' "Why not sit on my knees and have a crap?"

' "Not a bad idea, but I've thought of a better."

'And with that he goes to a towel cupboard and - whatever do you think? – gets out a cane and starts swishing it. A mean job it was – thin and whippy.

' "I always keep a cane handy in every room in the house," he says, "you never know when you may be needing one. Now then, darling Beatty: naughty little girls who use the Head's private bathroom, without asking permission first, have to be punished. But naughty Headmasters who climb up ladders to look at rorty little girls on the lav also have to be punished." He lets his trousers slither down and his pants after. Pretty legs he has. His stiff whichwhat curves down instead of up. Pervy, thinks I. "Bare botties," he is telling me. "Will you have the first whack, or shall I?"

'He's blocking the door. No way out. Shout for help? There's such a din coming up from all the piss artists you might as well shout from the bottom of the sea. "Rightie," says I, "let's get this straight. How many strokes before this charade is over?"

' "Three each",' he says. "Then I'll let you go. Done?"

' "Done."

' "But you must get it exactly right. Before every stroke you say to me, 'Dirty Master Peter, nanny saw him playing with it.' Then you swipe me as hard as you can. Then you say, 'One day it will come off, and Master Peter will have to

215

'... and that bastard Seagrams, he gets the window wide open ...'

carry it everywhere he goes, or he won't be able to do his little jobs.'"

' "Christ," I say. "And what do you say while you're whacking me?"

' "You'll find out."

'So I take first wallop,' says Beatty on the terrace while the nightingale sang ...

> (Hark! Ah, the nightingale ...
> The tawny-throated!
> Hark, from that moonlit cedar what a burst!
> What triumph! hark! ... what pain!)*

'... and I obey my instructions word for word. "*Dirty* Master Peter, nanny saw him playing with it." Wha-a-ack. Then, "One day it will fall off, etc. etc." Then it was my turn to be caned.

' "Bend over, Alicia," says Seagrams. "I want you to know that this gives me very great pleasure indeed, whacking you on your plump little twelve-year-old botty, *not* because I am a sadist but because I know I am doing the Lord's work in punishing your flagrant wickedness. Next time you want to masturbate, use your hairbrush handle and not one of the school First XI cricket bails. The start of today's cricket match was delayed twenty minutes while we looked for a spare one."

' "Jesus," says I, "are you going to use all that spiel every time you take a pot at my bum?"

' "No," he says, "something quite different each time."

And then, Wha-a-a-ack.

' "Alicia," he says, "your gay little *fesses* are quivering like black currant shape."

* From *Philomela*, by Matthew Arnold

217

'Then it's my go and I do my speech again. Then him for his second shot.

'"Alicia," he booms – and his voice is really deep and serious, no joking now – "if you continue in this abominable habit you will go to hell. Did you hear me? *To hell*."

'Wha-a-a-a-ack.

'Then my third and last chance to thump the bowling. I must say this for Seagrams. He's got a lovely pink, pert *derrière* on him. The red stripes across it made quite a subtle contrast of colours.

'But now it's him again. Last shot.

'"Oh God," he cries, all solemn and sombre, "I pray for the soul of this Thy servant Alicia Condamine, pupil of this school, who has this day defiled one of the school First XI cricket bails."

'Wha-a-a-a-ack. He then starts deftly feeling me up with the tip of the cane, but I reckon I've fulfilled my contract.

'"Must let me out," I tell him. "The game's over."

'"Fair enough," says he. He yanks up his knickers and his slacks, tucks his hyperbolical curve away to the left, unlocks the door, opens it, and bows me out like a princess, grinning all over his cherubic face. Now, what in Hades do any of you make of this Alicia Condamine bit?'

'She wasn't a pupil,' said JBB. 'Jonty told me about her. She was one of the science mistresses that came and went last year. Seagrams was particularly keen on her because she did some complicated trick with test tubes and a retort. One day the trick went wrong – or rather the retort did – and she had to leave. In an ambulance. But all this business of cricket bails is quite beyond me.'

'It must be a combination of fantasies,' I conjectured. 'Seagrams always likes to see adult women as little girls and vice versa. And somewhere in the middle of it all is genuine guilt. Didn't Beatty say that he was quite solemn and serious

218

for some of the time?'

'I did,' said Beatty. 'Like a priest giving the blessing. He has a beautiful voice for that kind of thing.'

Lucrezia came swaying along under the moon, her queenly robes flowing.

'What did you do with your court dress,' I enquired of Beatty, 'while Seagrams was caning you?'

'I pulled it up over my head.'

'Oh.'

'Lucrezia,' said Beatty, 'Seagrams has insulted me. I ought to go home at once as a protest.'

'Bet you enjoyed every second. Anyway, we can't go home because I've lost my panties. Has anyone seen my panties? I can't imagine why I bothered to wear them. One really doesn't need panties with long court dresses. But as I *was* wearing them, I must find them before we go home. They were a present from the children for Christmas. "You're always losing your panties, Mummy," they said so sweetly, "so here's a lovely big box with two dozen pairs." And talking of my children,' Lucrezia said, 'have you all heard the news about Torquil? Seagrams has gone and got him the third scholarship at Rugby. Torquil says they worked through all the papers together for the last three days before the exam. Really, you'd have thought more Headmasters would be up to that.'

'The Lord of the Isle is privileged,' said JBB. 'As my brother Peter, who knows the prep school game from alpha to omega could tell you, it is listed as "remote". Otherwise Torquil's papers would never have been sent here. Torquil would have had to go to Rugby to do the exam.'

'Yes, darling, that's rather what I thought. Seagrams is a bit of a rotter. The trouble is, Torquil is really quite dim.' She took a long suck at a tumbler and belched a cloud of gin. 'So what's going to happen is, they're going to find out before the first week is done that he ought *not* to be the third scholar, that he knows little Latin and far less Greek, that his maths are ex-ex-execrable, and that his French begins and ends with "*Où est le lavabo?*", and even that, I believe, is incorrect. So what, darlings, are they going to say? Are they going to say, "Torquil Lippit is a nasty little greaser?" or, "Peter Seagrams is a cunting great con-artist?" And *what* are they going to do about it?'

Jonty Delaware loomed along the terrace, his auburn hair, short though it was, much deranged.

'Seagrams has gone loony,' he said. 'He's got a sudden thing about hair. He's trying to cut everybody's off. Izzy and Jimmie are getting quite annoyed. Did I hear Lucrezia getting worried about Torquil at Rugby?'

'Yes, you did, doll,' said Lucrezia. 'What's going to happen to him?'

'Nothing,' said Jonty. 'Seagrams is a contemptible and pathological cheat, and so this sort of thing has occurred several times since I've been here – usually to the sons of rich, smart and beautiful women like yourself. The public schools, particularly the important ones like Rugby, hate admitting they've been made fools of, so they'll carry Torquil for a month or so, and then they'll have the school doctor in, and he'll discover that the eighteen-month-old Torquil was dropped on his nut by a drunken nanny while you were out for the evening. Of course the nanny didn't tell you, and Torquil just forgot, but although no one knew it he's never been quite right since. So nobody's really to blame, and he'll be quietly parked in the Army class or wherever they keep their morons these days.'

'Don't call my son a moron.'

'Sorry. I meant, wherever they keep boys that have been dropped on their heads by drunken nannies.'

'But won't they ask for an explanation of his scholarship papers?'

'They'll know the explanation.'

'Then won't Seagrams be punished?'

'There's no punishment left for Seagrams. He's already been thrown out of the IAPS.'

'But at least ... no one will send him scholarship papers any more?'

'Darling Lucrezia. Seagrams has been playing cricket and other games with masters from every major public school since he was knee-high. At Wellesley House, at Shrewsbury, at Oxford, while he was in the Guards, darling Lucrezia, and ever since, he's got to know scores, even hundreds, of men who are now running the entire public school circus. They all know what a shit Seagrams is and they all love him, because he makes them laugh. Their lives would hardly be tolerable without a new Seagrams enormity to laugh at every month or two. So papers for scholarships and everything else will go on being sent to him until the Lord of the Isle sinks into the lake or into bankruptcy, and that's all about that.'

'But you say these public schools hate being made fools of. So how can they possibly allow Seagrams to go on making fools of them?'

'But that's the whole point, darling. They don't allow him to make fools of them. As soon as they get a dud like Torquil, they pull in a doctor or someone similar to explain it all away.'

'Rather a waste of the scholarship money, when it might have gone to really clever boys.'

'So they might have thought once. But these days they're afraid of really clever boys. They are an embarrassment and a nuisance. They require a lot of work to be done on them. If they don't get tremendous awards at Oxford and

Cambridge, their parents complain like fuck. Double, double, toil and trouble – that's what clever boys mean. Much better have a nice, cosy number like Torquil, who'll sit in the Army class till the last trump and ask for nothing more than his daily wank.'

Along the terrace came a conga chain. Stroppington, hip-wagging like a houri, Jimmie bawling the music like a Wurlitzer, chunky, clownish Busker, Izzy the Ice Cream Man with half his hair chopped of, Seagrams, clacking a huge pair of kitchen scissors in time to the music, Vity and Vanushka, a whole row of young Trogs (including my brother, Myles, who was still with us then), Milesy Malbruges, miraculously balancing his backgammon set on his head, Spotty Birch, the Indian with the horizontal teeth. Beatty now hooks on to the Indian ('I love a bit of brown now and then'), Jonty on to Beatty, Lucrezia on to Jonty ('You gorgeous rugger-bugger, you'), JBB on to Lucrezia, the General on to JBB, and myself on to the General.

'The Troggy-Woggy Conga,' bellows Jimmie (who must already have been planning his suicide), 'Oh the Troggy-Woggy Conga – Ti-Ra-Ra-*rah*, Ti, Ra, Ra, *rah* . . . '

And so down the sloping lawn under moon and into the pavilion, where there is a barrel of beer waiting and a dozen of champagne.

'Seagrams, our host,' the toast goes up, 'Seagrams of the Lord of the Isle: *Seagrams*, with three times three.'

July 1987, Selsted by Canterbury

'Yes, they were great days at the Lord of the Isle,' said JBB on the boundary at Selsted, 'great days and jolly days, but of course they couldn't last.'

'The Trogs seem to be going on pretty well as it is,' said Lazarus Risen Plumb, 'if you'll pardon an outsider for saying so.'

'No outsiders,' said JBB. 'Anyone who has played in a Trog match or watched one becomes a member if he wishes. My brother, Peter, will sell you a tie for ten guineas.'

'I have a spare one,' said the Chancellor. 'I'll sell it to you for five.'

Lazarus ignored this. 'Where was your brother Peter,' he says to JBB, 'on that night at the Lord of the Isle? I don't remember his being mentioned.'

'Just that one year he went courting . . . on a holiday in Wales.'

'What happened?'

'She was too slack to walk up the last few hundred yards of Snowdon. So he decided against marriage.'

'A somewhat . . . captious reason?'

'It has sufficed him ever since.'

'And those that *were* there that night? What happened to them – those of them that are not here today?'

'Going down the conga chain,' said JBB. 'Stroppington has aged thirty years in twenty and no longer leads the dance; Jimmie soon became bored with being the life and soul of the party, and left it abruptly; Busker is happily married with an uncountable family; and Izzy the Ice Cream Man is a somewhat dodgy millionaire who has yet to run out of dodges. Peter Seagrams dissipated his patrimony and then

his entire school in acts of kindness, then vanished like a
wraith from a cruise boat in the Mediterranean. There are
those that think he may yet turn up again one summer
noonday, unannounced, to play cricket for the Trogs, which
was always what he loved most. Vity and Vanushka still live
in the Lake District, endlessly hospitable and doing good by
stealth. Of the young Trogs behind them, some still come
to play for us (though none is here today), others have
vanished forever into noxious cities, or prisons, or black
Hades. Milesy Malbruges still contrives a living of a kind
out of backgammon – we saw him at work not long ago at
Vity and Vanushka's. Spotty Birch has developed into a
probation officer of rather a ... specialised ... kind. The
amiable Indian with the horizontal teeth went back to
Mother India, where he married a Madrasi film star: clearly,
he had something going for him: when he had Beatty in the
trees outside the pavvy that night, she screamed like a
banshee for ten whole minutes. Beatty herself is big in
advertising or women's journals – I am never quite sure
which. Jonty Delaware now suffers from an ill-defined sense
of guilt to do with Seagrams: we can none of us be sure
whether he feels guilty because he once assisted Seagrams,
or because, in the end, he left him. We hope to see him
before the end of this tour, but he has for long been wary
of playing with the Trogs because, as he says, he feels that
Seagrams moves unseen among us, and this makes him
uneasy.

'Lucrezia Lippit lives near Vity and Vanushka. One day,
she told me, they all of them went to visit the Lord of the
Isle (long after Seagrams' death) during the school summer
holidays. They were kindly received by the Headmaster and
his wife, and found everything neat and well tended: the
lavatories were immaculate, the science labs had been rebuilt
(no possibility of an accident with the retort these days), the

terraces on the lawn had been sown with flowers and adorned with comfortable seats. But the old pavilion, the one in which we drank Seagrams' health, had been replaced by a slick new one with a well-signed convenience (no one need ever more go behind a tree or up to the school), and all the heart of the place was gone with it.

'The last three in the chain were myself, the General, and the Raven here. The Raven and myself, we are as you see us: the General has gone to answer the trumpet which summons all Lancers at the last.'

'And Dindyma, the girl who took care of James, who showed her tits to the whole island in order to get away from home?'

'She was in Cambridge the other day,' said James, 'and looked me up in Peterhouse. She is now a lecturer at the London School of Economics ... a fierce feminist in her late thirties, who looks as if she washed her hair in scrubbing soap.'

September 1987, Walmer

A last word. Of those not accounted for by JBB on that afternoon at Selsted in July, I should say that the Chancellor vanished suddenly from the tour after three days (having previously advertised his attendance for ten). This was possibly because he was lusting for the Lithuanian mistress whom JBB would not let him bring with him, but more probably because the computer, which nowadays assists his 'research', started to predict a Second Coming of Jesus Christ in the Lebanon (or so he wrote in apology to JBB), a phenomenon that would require immediate attention as it would very soon deprive journalists and people like the Chancellor of their main source of repute and livelihood ... in order to preserve which they would need to show the Prince of Peace a speedy exit.

Major Lazarus Risen Plumb walks up and down the earth from race meeting to race meeting, taking in other sporting events when the racing is too distant or dismal to get his attention. I saw him at Goodwood during the late August meeting.

'Whatever next?' he said to me. 'Lord March has already introduced evening meetings in his efforts to suck up to the proletariat and hoover their money. I suppose we shall be having slot machines in the paddock next, or nudie shows behind the Tote.'

Colonel O. 'Parafit' Paradore did not try to get his revenge on me at backgammon during the Trogs' tour as he was too happy in the company of Lazarus Risen to leave him for the board. But he did at last accept (earlier this month) my invitation to dine and play in my club. He now owes me well over £3,500 and shows no enthusiasm for paying it. The excuse he proffers is that he incurred his losses when in drink: whose fault was that? And finally, Master James Budden. He plans to join several more dining clubs during the ensuing academic year, and has hopes of a moderate second in part II of the Classical Tripos ... after which, he tells me, he will probably take a sabbatical year in order to decide what to do next.